Drover's Bounty

When a card game goes awry, drover Sam Hall wrestles with proficient gunslinger J.D. Seldon and when the pistol goes off Seldon is killed. After collecting the $500 bounty on Seldon's head, Hall travels to Wichita where he is befriended by a young Wyatt Earp and meets an enchanting young woman.

But J.D.'s older brother, Ben, is bent on revenge and has issued his own bounty on Sam Hall's head. With gunslingers and hardcases dogging Sam's every move, there is only one way out of this situation. He must find, and face down, Ben Seldon. . . .

Drover's Bounty

J.L. Guin

A Black Horse Western

ROBERT HALE · LONDON

© J.L. Guin 2013
First published in Great Britain 2013

ISBN 978-0-7198-0921-7

Robert Hale Limited
Clerkenwell House
Clerkenwell Green
London EC1R 0HT

www.halebooks.com

Typeset by
Derek Doyle & Associates, Shaw Heath
Printed and bound in Great Britain by
CPI Antony Rowe, Chippenham and Eastbourne

CHAPTER 1

Sam Hall counted his money before stuffing the wad in his shirt pocket. He and his fellow twelve drovers had just been paid off after having delivered the B bar B herd to Ellsworth, Kansas. They had been on the trail a little over three months and were ready for some time off. He and the others busied making ready to go to town for some rest and relaxation. Sam stuffed his dirty laundry into a saddle-bag. He shook out his bedroll then rolled it up and tied it behind his saddle cantle.

Daniel Helms, who stood nearby cinching his saddle tight, had noticed Sam's activity. 'Are you going some-where, Sam?'

'I need to get these things washed; I figured someone in-town could do that.'

'Well, it looks like you have everything you own tied on that horse,' Daniel noted.

Sam glanced over to Daniel. 'I like to stay foot loose. The drive is over. It's a long way back to Corpus Christi and I don't figure that the B bar B will need many hands for the winter. Most likely they won't have a need for a waddy until next spring's roundup. I've been thinking of looking around a bit; see some new territory; maybe find something to do besides painting houses and splitting firewood in the off time.'

Daniel chuckled. 'Seems you did all right painting Betty Hodges' house. How come you didn't move right in?'

Sam grinned. 'Oh, she wanted me to. That's a fact. I liked Betty; she was good company but it seems she had a few strings attached.'

Daniel looked enquiringly at Sam.

'She started pushing one day; marriage and adoption of those two kids of hers for starters. I liked the kids but I don't need a ready-made family. Besides, I found out that she has a sizeable note against that little spread of hers. I didn't see how it could work out on cowboy wages so I left out the front door and that bank clerk, Luther Grimm, came in the back. A month later they were married. I do hope it works out.'

'Hell, Sam, half the crew of the B bar B visited Betty before you came along. You lasted longer than any of them.' Daniel smirked. Sam didn't want to talk about old happenings so he changed the subject.

'What about you, Daniel, any plans?'

'I haven't thought that far ahead. I guess I have no long range plans. I'll likely spend most of this herding money in the next day or so. For now I just want to get to town and get started. I'm going to do some drinking, smoking, gambling and gabbing, then later on tonight I'm going to find one of those young pretties and allow her do some of those disgraceful things everybody's been talking about. Come tomorrow, or the next, I'll most likely be close to

6

broke and go on back with the others. B bar B sow belly and beans ain't so bad. At least I'll be eating.'

Sam and Daniel stepped into their saddles and headed the animals toward town.

Sam Hall's actual name was Samuel Hallingdal. He had shortened his name to Sam Hall a few years before for no other reason than simplicity. When he first signed on to herd cattle, the foreman was having trouble spelling Samuel. The man insistently wrote Samule and then was having trouble listing all the letters in Hallingdal so Samuel merely listed his name as Sam Hall. He was thirty-two years old, solidly built at 175 work-hardened pounds. His sandy hair and blue-gray eyes were taken from his Norwegian parents. He could shoot a rifle or a six-gun accurately as well as any of his counterparts, but his strength was in his fists. He was good with them, proven by the few scraps or misunderstandings he had with others that usually ended with Sam standing over his opponent.

Sam was a hard working cowboy who had never quite found a home. He would sign on to one of the many southern Texas ranches for the roundup and subsequent trail drive up the Chisholm Trail to one of the cattle shipping points such as Wichita or Abilene.

In years past, Abilene had been the preferred destination the Eastern cattle buyers had encouraged many Texas cattle owners to make as their shipping destination. That all changed in December of 1872. For four years Abilene had prospered as the number one shipping point. The prosperity also attracted a population of fly-by-night misfits who frequented Texas cattle towns. Saloons opened gambling tables and hired women to entertain lonely

7

cowboys that were set on painting the town red. Whiskey flowed like a waterfall and, as a consequence, the money the hard-working cowboys had taken three months to earn was sometimes squandered in a night or two of gambling and drinking. Wild six-gun shooting, fights, murder and thievery had come to town along with the herds. The city fathers of Abilene wanted their city to be the hub of trading for the numerous surrounding farms; they wanted a clean, progressive town that would attract both settlers and investors. At first grateful for the influx of business, they soon grew tired of the mayhem that the cattle trade thrust upon them and tried to correct things. They hired Wild Bill Hickok as city marshal to quell the violence on the streets. Hickok did too good a job. He quieted things down for a time, but ended up in a gun fight, regarding a woman, one fall evening. When the smoke cleared from Hickok's six-gun, his own deputy lay dead along with another man. Both had been shot by Hickok – the deputy by mistake.

The city fathers formed an organization that called themselves the Farmer's Protective Association of Dickinson County to rid the town of all the debauchery. They discharged their gunslinger marshal then sent a memo to be published in a number of Texas newspapers, in the winter of 1872, to the effect that no more cattle trading would be done in Abilene. The days of Abilene being a major shipping point for Texas cattle were over.

When the owner of the Drover's Cottage, which had been specifically built for the use of cattle buyers, cattle-men and cowboys, got the word that no more cattle would be trailed to Abilene he had the cottage dismantled, loaded on flat cars and sent sixty miles west to Ellsworth to be reassembled.

It was near mid-June in 1875 when the B bar B outfit from deep in southern Texas, near Corpus Christie, had finished the northward drive up the Chisholm Trail to Ellsworth.

Sam and Daniel boarded their horses in a livery. They bought new clothes, then booked rooms at the Drover's Cottage and cleaned themselves, readying for a little wildness and maybe a little wickedness. Their expectations were not great, just a night of relaxed drinking, a few card games and later to pay a visit to one of the out of sight houses inhabited by the soiled doves.

Things got off to an abrupt start when they left the confines of the hotel and stepped out the front door on to the board walkway. Anxious to get that first drink, they walked the wooden walkways heading to the first saloon they saw which was the Lucky Lady. All of a sudden the batwings of the saloon flew open. A beefy man in a white waist apron appeared through the opening. He dragged behind him a scruffy-looking smaller man, face down, held by his shirt collar. Once outside the building the beefy man jerked the smaller man up by the collar and belt then threw him into the street. The man plopped to a heap in the dusty roadway then began squirming to sit up.

'They're serving free drinks over at the horse trough!' the aproned man jeered. A dozen onlookers gave a chorus of cackled laughter. 'Damn bums don't even ask to work for it; they expect it for nothing,' the presumed bartender declared, then turned and went back inside the saloon followed by the grinning crowd.

The scruffy man, down in the dirt, managed to get to his feet. 'Sons-a-bitches,' he muttered, as another man of similar looks came to place a hand on his shoulder. 'Come on, Charlie, I got change in my pocket; it'll be enough for both of us.' The two shuffled off toward a different saloon.

Sam and Daniel followed the others inside the Lucky Lady to get their drinking day started. They seated themselves at an empty table, ordered a bottle of rye and had a drink then another and another, whiling away the afternoon gabbing to others. Daniel was a tall, strapping young man of 27 and blessed with good looks. He considered himself a ladies man, at least with prostitutes; that was true as long as he kept spending his cash on them. He had said many a time around smoky camp-fires that a good drink of whiskey and a bed woman were the finer things offered in life. It wasn't long before a chunky brunette wearing a bright red, split at the knee satin dress was sitting on Daniel's lap fingering the hair around his nape. He ran a hand up her dress without protest; she didn't flinch until he gave her a lick on the neck then whispered something into her ear. She stood abruptly, apparently not liking Daniel's proposition. 'I don't think so, cowboy,' she said, then walked away to the back of the room. Daniel merely laughed and poured another drink. Before long it was well past six o'clock and the two drovers were feeling no pain.

At Sam's insistence they made their way to a nearby restaurant for a meal of steak, mashed potatoes and gravy. After eating and somewhat sobered by the meal, they walked to a different saloon, The Golden Bull. It had a cavernous interior with a room-length bar on the left and numerous tables to the right mostly filled by groups of jawing cowboys and dealers flicking cards. Sam and Daniel sided up to the bar and ordered drinks.

Later on Daniel declared, 'Let's go over to Rita's house,' which was a well-known brothel that sat behind the saloons. When they got close they discovered half a dozen others standing around out front gabbing; some in the process of either rolling new smokes or puffing on ones already built. 'They are busy tonight,' a grinning cowboy said when Daniel and Sam approached. Daniel turned to Sam. 'Come on, I know another place; I ain't waiting in line behind these yokels.' Daniel began walking into the shadows of the now darkened roadway.

When they had gone a city block away they came to a shabby looking darkened building with low lamplight glowing through two windows. The place looked like it had been a stable at one time, now used to house low-class chippies. When Daniel turned to go to the front door Sam reached out and put a hand to Daniel's arm. 'This looks like a good place to get a whore's disease,' Sam cautioned.

'I've been here before, these girls are all right, cheaper too,' Daniel laughed, then opened the door and they walked in. Inside was a spacious room lined with couches that were covered with cloths, like sheeting. The back wall had three open doorways curtained with burlap for privacy. Two dark-eyed girls no older than eighteen or twenty sat cross-legged and expressionless on one of the couches. One curled her hair with a finger while the other just sat looking at the floor. They didn't bother to get up.

An older woman, of maybe thirty-five years wearing a brownish muslin dress came out from one of the curtained doorways. She was mid-height, perhaps 5' 6", slender of build with brown hair to her shoulders. She wore no make-up but had a friendly smile. She walked over to stand in front of Daniel. 'You want a girl?' she asked.

Daniel laid a hand on her shoulder and the two walked to the middle curtained door. The woman made an attempt to close the burlap curtain as she went in, but it remained half open. Sam watched as the woman sat on a bed then leaned back on to a pillow and raised the front of her dress. The two younger girls sat silently on their couch, expressionless, never making eye contact with Sam. It was like they had smoked opium or something and seemingly totally uninterested. Sam went outside to wait. He rolled a cigarette and smoked. When he threw the butt away Daniel walked out. 'Two dollars well spent!' Daniel proclaimed.

Later that night, inside the Golden Bull Saloon, Daniel stood at the bar, with his foot on a brass rail as he talked to two other men. Sam nudged Daniel with his arm. Daniel turned to look at him. 'I'm going to take that empty chair for a few hands,' he said and began to walk over to the table.

Daniel nodded his understanding. 'Better save some of your money if we're going back to try Rita's house a little later,' he advised.

Sam half turned. 'If I run out of money before then, I'd wager that you'd stake me.'

'If I got it,' Daniel grinned, then turned back to talk to the two men standing nearby.

'OK if I sit in?' Sam asked. When none of the five seated men objected he seated himself at the table.

'Your money is good here,' the dealer said. A portly man to Sam's left smiled broadly, 'Yeah, and he'll most likely get some of it before long.' He and two other men laughed. The other player remained silent, seemingly bored with the conversation.

The cards began falling in Sam's favor right away. He won the first hand and the next. After playing the following hand, the time came to reveal the winner. Sam turned his cards over, which included three aces, besting another player's pairs of jacks and nines.

'I've never lost three hands in a row, except to a cheat!' the unhappy man declared, then grated his chair back as he jumped to his feet. The man was young, perhaps early twenties, and of medium height and weight. He was cleanly dressed in black pants and boots with shiny buckles and spurs. He wore a ruffled white shirt covered by a black vest. A pair of white-handled silvery pistols rode in low-slung black holsters that braced his waist, the ends of the holsters tied to his legs. The man had neatly combed black hair that framed a sun-darkened swarthy face with close set black eyes. He had a scowl on his face as he pointed a finger at Sam. 'Let's see if you're just as lucky on the draw!' he declared.

Sam had stood and held his left hand, palm out, in an effort to dispel the outburst, for he had never cheated at cards. 'I did not cheat, mister!' Sam declared.

'Nobody's that lucky,' the agitated young man declared, then held his right hand over his six-gun. His hand trembled slightly; his right shoulder flinched, apparently in anticipation of a reaction from Sam. It didn't take long for Sam to figure that he would have to do something, and in a hurry. He was not a gun hand by any means. He carried his 1861 Army Colt pistol like any other cowboy did. It was there if needed to repel rustlers or Indians, or, if fired before a stampeding herd leader, it might turn or stop the beast. For the most part though, his six-gun was used very little.

When the man flinched his shoulder, Sam made a move. Instead of making an effort to draw his six-gun, he dived over the table at the man. He was quick enough to catch the man drawing his pistol clear of the holster but not yet leveled out. Sam's left hand locked the right wrist of the gunman holding the pistol muzzle downward. They fell into a heap as the gunman used his free left fist to pound Sam in the ribs again and again. Sam withstood the assault; his interest was in securing the gun the man was trying to draw on him. He held the gun hand firmly with his left hand while probing with his right to get a hold of the man's gun in the other holster. Just as he got a hand on it, the gunman pushed and rolled so that he lay on top of Sam. The move caused Sam to let go of the man's holstered gun and bring his right hand around to further secure the gun the muzzle of which the man was trying desperately to turn toward Sam. The two men lay chest to chest in the struggle with the six-gun wedged between them.

The suddenly quieted saloon patrons moved out of the way to stand and watch. The men kicking and struggling on the floor rolled one way then the other trying to gain an advantage. One more roll put Sam on top and then there was a distinct but muffled shot. The pistol between the two men had discharged. It was not an excessively loud shot, the muzzle being muffled by clothing and bodies. Everyone watched as the two men's frantic actions on the floor suddenly ceased. Smoke curled out between the two men's chests. For a moment nothing happened as the men lay locked together. No one could tell which man had been hit by the fired pistol. Slowly Sam pulled one hand free then the other. He placed his palms on the floor and pushed himself up to stand over the still form of the man who, just moments ago, had been attempting to shoot him. The gunman still clutched his shiny six-gun, at an odd angle, against his own chest. He lay without movement and his eyes closed. A rivulet of blood began inching along the floor away from the downed man's chest area.

Two men appeared from the depths of the saloon. One man knelt next to the fallen gunman. He probed a hand to look at the wound in his chest then felt the neck area for a pulse. Finding none he declared, 'He's dead.' The man stood and pointed a finger at Sam. 'You killed him! You murdered him!'

Sam, bewildered as he was over the fracas, stood in disbelief, but was not about to be rough handled or accused unjustly. 'Didn't you see what happened?' he demanded. 'He drew on me!'

Both of the two men stood facing Sam, arms at their sides, hands near holsters. They were too far away for Sam to try a repeat and dive for either one's gun hand. Sam allowed his right hand to brush against the top of his holster in an effort to get a reassuring touch of his six-gun. It was not there. The six-gun had come out of his holster during the fight and was lying somewhere on the saloon floor. Meantime Daniel had walked over and stood next to

Sam. Daniel did not say anything. He just stood eyeing the two men, letting them know that Sam was not alone. One of the men went for his six-gun that was held in a tied down holster on his thigh. Daniel reacted automatically with the quickness of a striking rattlesnake. He drew his six-gun in a heartbeat and fired before the other man's gun muzzle was level. The result was that the man's gun fired into the floor in front of Sam. The man fell backward, fatally wounded from the shot to the middle of his chest.

At the same instant, the stricken man's partner, a tall, gaunt man with dark hair, had drawn his six-gun and pulled the trigger at the same time that Daniel had fired. Daniel stood for a moment without moving. He attempted to holster his six-gun, but the muzzle of the pistol missed the holster and the gun dropped from Daniel's hand. He looked down as if to retrieve the fallen weapon then fell forward. Sam attempted to catch Daniel when he started to fall. They both ended up crashing into an empty table and chairs. The man who had shot Daniel, apparently figuring that his partner was done for, was last seen backing out the batwings with six-gun held at the ready. He disappeared into the night.

CHAPTER 2

Sam was kneeling over Daniel when the sheriff and a deputy arrived. The sheriff knelt over each of the prone men for a moment. When he was satisfied that nothing more could be done for them he stood, then turned to face Sam, who was standing nearby.

'Did you have a hand in this?' the sheriff asked.

Sam nodded. 'That one, a man I don't even know' – Sam pointed to the man in the black vest – 'accused me of cheating at cards. He drew a gun on me. I grabbed him before he could pull the trigger and we commenced to fight. The gun went off between us and he ended up shooting himself.'

'What about these other two, do you know them?'

'The one in the blue shirt is a drover. We're together. He came over to stand with me when that one' – he pointed to the man Daniel had outdrawn and killed – 'he and another man drew down on us. Daniel shot this one while the other man shot Daniel at the same time.'

'And you didn't shoot any of them?'

'As a matter-of-fact no, I didn't. My six-gun dropped out

17

during the scuffle and is still on the floor someplace.'

'Here it is,' a man standing nearby said, then reached under a table and picked up a six-gun and handed it toward Sam. The sheriff reached out and took the weapon and stuck it in his waistband.

'What about the other man, the one you say shot your friend. Where is he?'

'I guess I didn't see him leave, I was too busy trying to tend to Daniel.'

The sheriff turned to face the bartender, 'How about it, Mort? Do you know who the other man is?'

'He backed out the door while he was pointing that gun inside,' the bartender said. 'It was Leroy Hagen. Leroy, Larry and J.D. there, came in two, three hours ago.'

'Did you see what happened here?' the sheriff asked.

The bartender answered, 'You can ask Wilson if there was any cheating going on; he was the dealer at that table. I wasn't paying any mind to the dealings until J.D. started yelling out that he was cheated, otherwise, everything that this fella said is a fact. J.D. drew down on him and they got into a scuffle, the gun went off and J.D. got the bad end. Leroy and Larry came over and drew on that other fella who shot Larry, then Leroy shot him. Right after that, Leroy left.'

The sheriff looked around the room at the onlookers. 'Can anybody else add anything?'

A man in a brown suit spoke up. 'It's just like Mort said; this man didn't do anything other than win a few hands of poker. J.D. didn't like losing, I guess, so he jumped up and called this fella out. It looked to me that it was self-defense. That other fella, this man's partner got shot when those other two drew on him.'

The sheriff nodded his understanding then turned to his deputy. 'Duke, get some of these fellas here to help you get these bodies over to Jensen's undertaking.' He turned to face Sam. 'You come with me; I have a few more questions to ask.'

The sheriff led the way to the jail. He walked over and laid Sam's six-gun on his desk then stepped to a coffee pot. He poured half a cup and offered it to Sam. Sam took it. He poured himself a half cup then took a seat behind the desk. He opened a drawer and brought out a bottle of whiskey and held it up for Sam to step forward if he wanted some. He poured a generous amount into Sam's cup then filled his own. Sam sat in a chair facing the desk.

'A man ought to have something after a fiasco like that.'

'Thanks,' Sam acknowledged.

The sheriff opened a book with blank lined pages and took a pencil in hand. 'I'll need your name, the name of your dead friend and the outfit you're riding for.'

'It's Sam Hall. My friend's name was Daniel Helms. We were riding for Tom Blake's B bar B.'

The sheriff stuck a meaty hand over for a shake. 'I'm John Sikes. I took over after Sheriff Whitney was gunned down last year.'

The two men shook hands then Sikes went back to making entries in the book.

'Do you know who that fella in the black vest was?' he asked.

'No,' Sam answered slowly, 'I never saw him before tonight.

'Well, his name is J.D. Seldon,' John Sikes affirmed,

then muttered as if to himself, 'He finally got caught up with. I didn't even know he was in town.

'You here at the tail end of trail drive?'

'We just finished this morning,' Sam acclaimed.

'Where are you from?'

'I come from Texas, down Corpus Christi way. Don't rightly know if I'll go back there or not.'

'Let me guess, you're another wandering cowboy who just finished the drive, got paid, and you'll work for any outfit that will have you after your money runs out.'

'That's the way it's been the past few years, Sheriff. I didn't come into town to stir up any trouble.'

'I'm assuming that you didn't, however, the cards and drinking didn't mix very well and some men died as a result. That fact might prove to be a headache for you, later on.'

'What are you saying, Sheriff? Am I under arrest, or what?'

'No, there aren't any charges against you.'

'Are you going after the other one, uh, Leroy Hagen, is that his name?' Sam asked.

'I'd say you're lucky that Leroy didn't plug you too, but I think when he left he was looking out for his own skin rather than worrying about shooting someone on J.D.'s account. To answer your question, the answer is no: I won't be going after him. I don't believe that Leroy is a murderer and I don't rightly see that he purposely killed your friend. A jury would never convict him of such. It was not a planned killing. The witnesses, including you, say that three men shot at each other after a heated saloon brawl; two of those men died. Justifiable homicide it was;

it's as simple as that. Leroy is a small time thief; eventually he'll pull something that will be to his undoing.'

Sam was aghast by what he had just heard. 'Am I to let the boss know that he should tell Daniel Helm's relatives that he died at the hands of a man who won't even be charged for the killing? That the man may get caught someday on a different charge and that would be his just punishment?' Sam fumed.

John Sikes colored. He stared at Sam for a moment, perhaps in an attempt to refrain from shouting. He took a deep breath, then said in a low voice, 'It would be best if you don't get on a high horse on this matter. I know the law and I'm telling you that there isn't enough evidence to bring charges on the man!' He paused for a moment then muttered something under his breath to the effect of 'need to stay calm'. Sikes stood, picked up Sam's gun by the barrel and handed it to him, butt first. 'If you come over to the office tomorrow, I'll see that you get paid.'

'Get paid!' Sam was startled. 'For doing what?'

'For putting J.D. Seldon out of action,' the sheriff said. 'He had a five hundred dollar bounty on his head. He's been dodging the law for a long time. He spends his time gambling, drinking, stealing and has outgunned at least two men that I am aware of. About six months ago, they say, he and another man killed a newly married couple down near Little Rock, just to steal their horses and valuables. A reward was posted right after the incident. The citizens of two states will be grateful that his killing and thieving days are done,' the sheriff concluded. Sikes remained standing.

Sam nodded his understanding. 'That's a lot of money.

I've never had that much, at one time, in my entire life. I don't know why I should get the credit or blame for the man's death: he shot himself!'

'The reward is there if you want to claim it,' Sikes said curtly.

'Shouldn't the money go toward burying him?' Sam reasoned.

'I'm going to sell his horse, saddle and guns. That will more than cover the burial. What's left over goes into the city's kitty. If no one claims the reward then it just doesn't get paid,' Sikes said, then added, 'seems like a waste.'

It sounded to Sam that the sheriff was encouraging him to claim the reward money and the man seemed sincere about it. Sam rolled the thought around in his head for a moment. That amount of money would allow him to do a lot of things and not have to do nonsense jobs before next year's roundup. It was an opportunity for the taking so he said, 'If that's the case then I'll lay claim to it and come back tomorrow like you say.'

Sikes nodded. 'I'll send a wire out in the morning to the sheriff's office in Little Rock that I am verifying J.D. Seldon's identity and death. Once they send back the OK, I can then make the payout. All you have to do is sign for the money,' Sikes said. 'Come in after noon and maybe we'll have the answer by then.'

Sam turned and left the sheriff's office and made his way to his room at the Drovers Cottage.

CHAPTER 3

Leroy Hagen was worried when he backed out of the Golden Bull saloon. He wasn't afraid that someone would shoot him for he kept the batwings in view and his gun at the ready while making his way to his tethered horse, in the shadows nearby. What bothered Leroy was being the one who would have to tell Ben Seldon the news. For now though, he had to get out of town before someone tried to stop him.

He hastily mounted up and spurred the animal to a run out of town and into the darkness. After twenty minutes of galloping Leroy slowed the heated animal to a walk. It did not appear that anyone was following. Leroy had a long way to go and he didn't want to overly exert his horse. Thoughts filled his head about J.D's brother.

Ben Seldon was thirty-five years old, senior to J.D. by twelve years, and had more or less raised the youth after both their father and J.D.'s mother had died in a cholera outbreak. Ben's mother had run off with another man two years before his father took up with another woman who would later give birth to J.D. The family farm near Baxter

Springs, Kansas, located in the extreme south-eastern corner of Cherokee County provided but a meager existence for Ben and J.D; that is until Texans began driving their cattle herds through the area on their way to market in places such as Kansas City, Sedalia and St Louis.

At first, Ben had merely taken in three strays from a passing herd; the welcome cash from a quick sale to a butcher shop emboldened the young man to collect more and more trail tired cattle whenever drovers let their guard down. He soon figured out that to really take advantage of the situation, he needed help to increase the take. It wasn't long before Ben had recruited others who were not particularly concerned about the legality of the ownership of the cattle. He ruled the outfit with an iron hand. Any questioning of his plans or the share paid, was met with swift fists or a gun.

J.D. thirsting for fancy goods and excitement, wanted more than Ben was willing to give his younger half-brother. 'The money goes into the pot. You get as much as you need!' Ben had declared. J.D. had left in a huff six months previously and had been on the lam since. Ben had heard of the incident in Arkansas of which J.D. and another were accused. It wasn't that he didn't believe it for he knew that J.D. was capable of killing if someone got in his way. Hell, he'd done it himself. Thieving cattle was one thing, but out and out murder of strangers, well, he'd just have to postpone judgement on the matter until such time as he could talk to his brother himself. When Ben learned that J.D. was up in Ellsworth, he sent Leroy Hagen and Larry Brown to see if they could discover if J.D. had any thoughts of returning to his Kansas home.

Who could say what Ben would do once he learned of the death of his brother? Ben was known to fly off the handle and become belligerent for any incidental trifle. Leroy did not dare run off without telling Ben, knowing that he would come looking, once he received word. Leroy's only comfort was that it would take two days of riding before he would have to face him.

CHAPTER 4

Sam had spent a fitful night trying to sleep. He kept waking, his mind troubled. He lay awake for a long time before he arose around seven and went downstairs to the hotel restaurant for breakfast. He spotted Jim Lance, the trail boss of the B bar B, and one of his fellow drovers, Smithy Jones, seated at a nearby table. He walked over and stood before their table. Before anyone could even say good morning, Sam said, 'Daniel Helms was killed in a shootout last night over at the Golden Bull Saloon.'

A look of alarm went to Jim Lance's eyes then a blank look of resignation. He held a hand toward a chair. 'Sit down, Sam, and tell us about it.'

'You look kinda ruffled,' Smithy Jones commented. 'Musta been a rough night.'

'It was,' Sam said, as he pulled out a chair and sat down. Before breakfast was finished Sam had recounted the entire episode, including the reward offered by the sheriff.

'Are there any charges against you, Sam?' Jim Lance asked.

'No, there aren't any charges against me and none on

26

the man who shot Daniel either. The sheriff said there wasn't anything that the law could do. He said the deaths were justifiable homicide.'

'You gonna take the reward money?' Smithy asked.

'Yes, I'm going to take it. Why shouldn't I? That fella was going to kill me before Daniel stepped in,' Sam responded, 'Part of it will go to seeing that Daniel gets a decent burial. I'm going to the undertakers as soon as I leave here and make the arrangements.'

Jim Lance sat back in his chair. 'I am truly sorry to hear this about Daniel. He was a good man and did his job without complaint. I'd like to attend the funeral and I'm sure the rest of the boys would like to pay their respects as well. If you're making the arrangements just let us know what time it will be.'

'I will,' Sam said, then stood and walked out the front door.

Early that afternoon, Sam Hall stood before a bulletin board in the sheriff's office. He was looking over the Wanted posters tacked to the board. The sheriff nodded when Sam had come in, then busied working the dial on a heavy safe behind the desk. Soon the sheriff counted out $500 and he had Sam sign a receipt for the money before handing the cash to him.

The sheriff looked at the elated expression on Sam's face when he had handed him the cash. Sikes figured on giving Sam some advice, or a warning, to go along with the money. He pointed to the bulletin board. 'Man-hunting is a sorry game. Often times it ends up a bitter one for the hunter as well as the hunted. That money in your pocket might seem to have come easy, but that's not always the case. You seem like a decent enough man. If you have it in mind to go after any other wanted men, I'd say forget it.'

'I was just looking to see if there was a reward on Leroy Hagen,' Sam said.

'There is a two-hundred-dollar reward offered for Hagen for stealing a wagonload of sacked grain over in Missouri. Here, I'll give you a copy of that dodger.' Sikes handed him a copy and added, 'He and that J.D. sure did get around.' Still unsure of Sam's intentions, he asked, 'Are you planning on going after him?'

'If I knew where he went, I sure would. It would be the right thing to do for Daniel. I'll keep this paper as a reminder, just in case I ever run across him. You wouldn't happen to know where he hangs out would you?'

Sikes looked at him quizzically. 'If I knew, which I don't, I wouldn't tell you. He could be fast on the draw,' he cautioned. 'But that paper isn't a ticket to go and shoot someone. It doesn't say dead or alive. It's payable if he's brought in to answer to the charges.'

'Oh I won't be trying to outdo a quick-draw man. There are other ways to subdue someone.'

'Well, watch your step, anyway. There could be others who may be gunning for you,' the sheriff cautioned again.

'You mean friends of that fella J.D.?' Sam asked.

'Oh I wouldn't call anybody J.D.'s friend. He didn't have any real friends. He was a rat and ran with a rough bunch. He did as he pleased without the help of anyone that I know of. You can be sure though that Leroy Hagen ran straight to J.D.'s brother Ben to tell of the shooting. Those who know him say that Ben is just as mean and nasty as J.D. was. Ben is not known for being as fast on the draw as his brother, but it's been said that Ben might shoot you from ambush. Ben could be looking for some sort of revenge and he might drag Leroy along just to identify the man who caught J.D. I'd say it's a strong possibility for you to consider. Aside from vengeance from Ben, what I'm talking about is someone who is looking for a name for hisself. J.D. Seldon was a notorious gunman. Word will get out that you were faster on the draw than he was and that makes you the man to beat. If someone should outdraw you then he gets bragging rights.'

'But I didn't draw on him,' Sam explained, 'he drew on me.'

'You know it; I know it, and everyone at the Golden Bull last night saw what happened. I also know how folks are; how they talk and get things a little mixed up. The more they talk the more the story will be embellished and twisted. Why, by the end of the week folks will be saying that there was a gunfight and you out-drew J.D., plain and simple.'

'Does everybody need to know my name?' Sam asked.

'Anyone involved in a death has his name listed in county ledgers. The law requires it and the ledgers become a public record. The newspaper people have access to the records. You can just about count on it; *The Ellsworth Reporter* will have a story out on the shootings, most likely, by tomorrow morning.'

Sam nodded his acknowledgment and turned to leave. Sheriff Sikes made one final appeal. 'If you stick around town, word will get out and sooner or later someone will no doubt call you out. Do you understand, Sam?' he asked. 'It would be best if you go far and wide from here, right away. Don't even spend the night in town. Fact is, unless you're willing to sit in your hotel room until your outfit is set to leave, I'm ordering you to leave town! If Ben Seldon is intent on getting at you then the first place he'll be looking is right here where the incident happened. Why don't you go back to cattle herding? Forget about Leroy. Go on home and do it today!'

'I'm leaving town about four o'clock as soon as the funeral for Daniel is over,' Sam advised. He turned and walked out the front door. He made a right turn and headed for the livery to check on the care of his horse and to pay his bill. He had walked maybe thirty paces when he happened to notice two men across the street, one of whom pointed at him. They appeared to be in conversation and watched as he walked along. He also noticed a man sitting in a chair on the boardwalk. The man looked in Sam's direction then stood abruptly and hurried inside a building as if to avoid a confrontation. Two other men were standing nearby, obviously local farmers, for they were dressed in bib overalls, brogans and wore slouch hats. They watched as Sam approached. One man spoke when Sam neared. 'Say ain't you the fellow who had that shootout with J.D. Seldon last night?'

Sam stopped and looked at both men for a moment, then decided to set the facts straight hoping that they would pass the information on. 'There was no shootout,' Sam informed him. 'The man tried to draw on me. I jumped him before he finished the draw. We had a scuffle and he pulled his own trigger. Fortunately the bullet hit him instead of me.' The men stood silent; one held his mouth open as if greatly surprised. Sam turned and resumed his walk to the livery. He led the roan over to The Old Reliable House, a mercantile that carried about anything a man could imagine. In a cotton sack a clerk placed a small coffee pot, a fry pan, a small bag of flour, a two pound chunk of bacon and two bags of smoking tobacco. He filled a small bag of ground coffee beans that he emptied from a grinder. Sam took the merchandise and tied the bundle, wrapped it with his rain slicker and secured it behind his cantle. He left the horse while he went to the Drovers Cottage to settle his bill.

All the B-bar-B cowboys were in the hotel's saloon waiting for the time to go to the graveyard. It was uncommonly quiet at the bar; most of the men were making small talk in low tones, or were silently staring into their drinks when Sam came in and ordered a beer. When he had drunk about half of it, a gaunt man in a black suit entered the saloon. He walked over to Sam and said in a soft but audible voice, loud enough for all to hear in the quieted room, 'We are ready to proceed with the service, sir.' Sam nodded and turned to follow. The other drovers quickly downed the remainder of their drinks then congregated outside on the boardwalk.

They watched as the black-suited man climbed to his seat in a weather-grayed wagon that had a black and silver sign hung on the side boards with *Jensen Undertaking* blazoned on it. In the bed of the wagon lay a freshly milled pine coffin, the top and sides of which were covered with a black satin cloth. The men mounted and followed the hearse, in its dreary slow pace to the cemetery a short distance from town. No one knew if Jensen was also a preacher, but the man spoke over Daniel's coffin for a long three minutes until finally, he announced 'Amen'. Willing cowboy hands grasped ropes to lower the box into the grave. Two workmen stood nearby, one man leaning on a shovel as he slouched and waited to fill the grave. The men stared blankly like vultures waiting for predators to leave a carcass so they could swoop in for their turn. Their clothing was rumpled and dusted brown with dirt, presumably from a rush of business as there were two other open graves, freshly dug, a few yards away.

After Daniel's funeral the men began walking toward their horses. Jim Lance turned and asked Sam, 'You were the closest to Daniel; do you know if he had any family who should be notified?

Sam thought for a moment. 'I met Daniel when you hired us both on the same day a few months ago. I liked him and we had become friends. I know everyone has a mother and father but Daniel never talked of any family life to me. One time, when we were huddled up on a rainy night in one of the trail camps, we heard someone say that they sure wished that they were back home next to a fire. Daniel just smiled, and said, "Why even this is better than where I come from!" Daniel and I herded cattle together; he was a good hand but when it came to his personal life, the man never elaborated on things like where he had come from, or where he had worked before.'

Jim Lance lifted his palm up in a questioning manner. 'We never feel the need to know a man's life history when he signs on to work cattle. I'll take Daniel's belongings and what money he had left, back to the ranch, and leave word to that effect at the sheriff's office in case anyone ever tries to locate him.' He turned and mounted his horse then looked to Sam. 'You ain't quitting, are you?'

'I've a few things to take care of, but I might see you in the spring,' Sam said.

'Is that money burning a hole in your pocket, or are you thinking of going after that fella who shot Daniel?' Lance asked.

'Somebody ought to; the law isn't going to do anything. Daniel didn't deserve to die like that,' Sam said. 'The reward money will give me a stake to get after him, if I choose to.'

'I hate to see you go off alone, could be mighty dangerous work but I hope you don't ask any of the crew to go with you; they'll be needed at the ranch,' Jim Lance said hopefully.

'I know that any one of them would follow along but this is something that I have to do myself. You needn't worry, Jim, I won't ask anyone.'

Jim Lance nodded then nudged his horse to a walk. He figured to himself that if Sam didn't get himself killed then it would take until spring for him to go through the cash that he had, and he wouldn't be surprised if the man showed up next spring looking for work.

Jim and the rest of the B-bar-B crew would spend another night in town then begin the return trip to the ranch in the morning. Sam said farewells and shook hands with all the men with whom he had spent months working and living, then mounted and rode out of town.

CHAPTER 5

Sam had not wanted to leave town so soon, or under the circumstance either. He had come into town wanting nothing more than a little rest and recreation. Now he was leaving scarcely twenty-four hours since he and Daniel had booked their rooms yesterday. He was tired and exasperated after last night and today's events. He knew he could not stay another night in Ellsworth. Even Sheriff Sikes had implored, then ordered him, to depart, perhaps in fear that Ben Seldon and Leroy Hagen might come to town seeking vengeance. It had been his first time in Ellsworth and he wasn't sorry to put the bad memory of the town behind him.

He longed for familiar surroundings and had the same events taken place in either Abilene or Wichita he most likely would have stayed on until morning. He had trailed herds to both towns in years past. Abilene was the closest from where he was, only about sixty miles away. He thought of riding there, but would get into town quite late if he did. He wondered what the place would be like since the Drover's Cottage had been moved to Ellsworth. A number of other establishments most likely followed right along. If cowboys were not welcome in Abilene three years ago then those responsible for that decision most likely had not changed their minds, so he would not go there now.

He put the roan to an easy lope heading south-east to Wichita. Uneasy thoughts began to invade his mind. Maybe there was something to Sheriff Sikes's warnings that J.D.'s brother Ben and Leroy Hagen might come after him. Sam Hall had never run from a fight and he did not like having to act like a hunted criminal. He tried to resist the urge to look back to see if anyone was following as he rode along but found himself occasionally turning to see. He tried to remember what Leroy Hagen looked like but things had happened so quickly that his memory had faded. He attempted to conjure in his mind the two men standing before him. The scornful look of the man who had pointed accusingly at him; the other, Leroy, a tall, gaunt-looking man with dark hair, but no image of the man's face came to mind. Hell, if someone was after him, they would be complete strangers. He tried to dismiss the thought before he became suspicious of every movement made by the wind.

Sam rode until dusk then stopped in a grove of cotton-wood trees that grew alongside a running creek. He stripped his saddle then hobbled the roan to munch cot-tonwood leaves and bark. After gathering some broken twigs and old dried branches he soon had a small camp fire going. Fried bacon, pan bread and boiled Arbuckle's coffee was the fare, the light cinnamon aroma of the coffee was comforting. He sat munching the simple meal as he thought to himself with disgust, I've got more money on me than I have ever had at one time and I can't spend a nickel of it. So here I sit eating trail food. 'Things will change come the morrow,' he muttered. When the meal was finished he laid aside his cup and eating utensils then rolled out his blanket and lay down. Sam looked at the stars briefly then fell into a deep sleep almost immediately. At the first hint of dawn with a tint of cream showing on the eastern horizon, Sam awoke and rekindled the fire, then made coffee. By full daylight he broke camp and allowed the roan to follow the creek toward Wichita situated next to the Arkansas River.

CHAPTER 6

Late in the morning, Sam reined his horse to a halt in the middle of the trail, on the west entrance facing the Douglas Avenue Bridge. On either side of him were ramshackle buildings housing dance halls and cathouses quiet at this time of the morning. Nighttime was when they came to life, becoming a rendezvous of the vile and wicked. Brightly lit and churning out laughter and music, the establishments welcomed those who would cross over from the prosperous east side. Sam walked his horse across the bridge then stopped to look down the street; there were a few new buildings, but it seemed as though he had never been away. The town dozed in the mid-morning sun exactly as he had remembered it from last year's trail drive. A number of horses drowsed at the hitch rails in front of false front businesses that lined both sides of the street.

A cowboy rushed out of a saloon, vaulted into the saddle of his nearby horse. He turned the horse on to the street, kicked it to a run, then began firing his pistol into the air as he rode out the other end of town. Those who were out when the shooting began, were apparently so used to the behavior that few hardly even looked up and none was seen jumping for cover. Sam muttered wryly, 'Hell, things ain't changed a bit.'

Just then a team pulling an empty wagon bolted down the street, perhaps frightened by the shooting, the horses running wild. Sam dug a heel to get the roan to a run, then guided his horse to the pace of the running team. He reached a hand over, grabbing the harness of one of the horses, then pulled hard on it while using his other hand to pull his own reins to the left. The move was enough to stop the agitated team.

A tall young man in a black suit coat with a badge pinned on his lapel, rushed into the street to take control of the team. Once he had the ribbon lines in hand and the horses were settled, the man turned to Sam and said, 'Thanks, mister, that could have been a real catastrophe.' Sam nodded to him then nudged the roan to walk over to face the Carey Hotel and saloon. He looped reins, grabbed his booted rifle and saddle-bags then walked into the hotel and booked a room. He stashed his belongings in the room then took his horse to the A One livery for care and feeding.

Sam walked the street for a time until he came to a sandwich board out front of Reed's Restaurant that read Meals 25 Cents. It was a small restaurant with only five tables, three of which were occupied, and a short counter standing before the kitchen area. A middle-aged woman came forward. 'Sit where you like.' Sam took a chair before an empty table. 'Coffee?' she asked. Sam nodded. He had a bowl of split pea soup pebbled with chunks of ham, some hot biscuits and plenty of strong black coffee. Afterwards he went to his room at the Carey Hotel for a short nap. Later he cleaned up using the provided pitcher of water and basin, then changed into clean clothes and readied for his delayed night on the town.

Sam spent an uneventful night wandering from saloon to saloon enjoying the drinks and small talk with drovers from arrived herds. He did not feel like going on a drinking binge; the whiskey was all right but it just wasn't the same as before. He didn't feel the need to get drunk and let off steam like the night he and Daniel Helms came to town. Somehow the fun of it had been lost. Perhaps he was apprehensive that a man or two might be looking to do him harm. It was as if he had suddenly grown up. He had no reason to be upset. He had more money than he imagined he would ever have and not a soul knew where he was. At least he had told no one of his destination when he had left Ellsworth and, as far as he knew, no one had followed him here. Wanting to enjoy himself Sam seated himself at a card game. He was watchful of those he played with because of the happenings in Ellsworth. After a few hands he relaxed somewhat and enjoyed the games.

CHAPTER 7

After the shooting in Ellsworth, Leroy Hagen had ridden all night. At first it was a frantic ride to get out of town, then slowed once a few miles were ridden. He took good care that none should ride behind him. Even in the moonlight Leroy knew where he was. He had been all over this country in past years, mostly as a trail hand delivering stolen cattle for Ben Seldon to customers who were not concerned at the brand on a steer's hide. He had made trips, many under the cloak of darkness, to Abilene, Wichita, Newton and, of late, to Ellsworth.

Once he had ridden across the Kansas River after leaving Ellsworth he headed in a south-easterly direction toward Newton. It would be a straight line to Newton and on to Ben Seldon's place near Baxter Springs. After a few hours of riding, Leroy stopped near a cluster of cottonwoods next to a shallow creek to give his horse a rest. He sat around munching some saddle-bag jerky until he began to get cold. Not seeing the worth of building a camp-fire that could easily be spotted, he strained to look in the darkness for any hint of followers. Satisfied that

40

there were no pursuers, Leroy mounted and continued his journey.

He breathed a sigh of relief when he entered Newton shortly after dawn. Now he could get a meal and rest the horse and himself for a while. He checked his horse into a livery then walked to a little café that had a sign out front offering all you can eat for 25 cents. He had coffee, biscuits and gravy. Stuffed and lethargic, he stood out front of the café and rolled a smoke while trying to think of a way to break the news of J.D's demise to Ben. It's still a long way to Baxter Springs and it just happened last night, he reasoned to himself. No sense getting in a hurry; hell, there wasn't anything he, or Ben for that matter, could do about J.D. now. He'd done what he could, he shot one of them. So what if the other one got away? Ben would be upset, but telling him could wait, he figured. Leroy went back to the livery and lay down in a straw covered stall next to his own horse's stall. He was tired and figured the livery operator wouldn't mind.

CHAPTER 8

Sam slept until past daylight, unusual for him. He splashed some water on to his face, from a pitcher and basin in his room then ventured down to the hotel restaurant for breakfast. He decided to spend the day shopping for new equipment. He didn't need a new saddle as his was only a year old. He did buy a new saddle blanket and a bridle, both of his being well worn. He took the goods to the livery. While there he had the smith check over the roan's shoes, then rubbed the animal down and fed him. Next he went to Jones's Mercantile where he bought a new India rubber slicker as his old one was dirty and trail worn.

A trip to the gunsmith was next. When Jock Avery, the owner of the shop, learned that Sam was interested in a new six-shooter he began a practiced sales speech. 'That old 1861 Army Colt cap and ball pistol you got there needs to be retired. The caps most likely misfire about twenty per cent of the time – a hundred per cent if you get those paper cartridges wet while crossing a river. These new six-guns are fast loading and take a sealed cartridge. The cap and powder are sealed in a metal shell with the bullet already attached. Why, you can take the gun and ammo right into the river water and come out the other side and fire all six rounds without a failure. I'm surprised that you never had that one converted. It costs about twelve dollars to do, but you'd be better off with a new gun anyway.' Avery handed a single action Peacemaker .45 over the counter for Sam's inspection. 'That's the most popular model that I deal with.' He laid six cartridges on the counter. 'Step out back and shoot a few targets. I know you'll like the feel of that Colt.'

Sam loaded the cylinder then stepped through the back door. The targets were placed at twenty yards, thirty yards, seventy-five yards and a hundred yards. Sam blasted away at the nearer targets figuring the others were for rifle practice. He walked out and looked at the effects of his shooting. Satisfied he returned to the counter.

'It's twenty-seven dollars; a new holster is three dollars and I'll throw in a box of cartridges.' Sam was busy emptying the spent shells from the pistol and did not answer the man right away. The gunsmith pushed for a conclusion, 'You can get it cheaper by mail order but this one is available right now. I can take your old Colt in trade; 'course it isn't worth much.' His voice trailed off.

'I'll take it and the holster and three boxes of cartridges.' Sam strapped on the new holster then practiced a few draws to see that the gun did not stick in the holster too tightly. He paid the man then left.

In the afternoon, Sam lounged in a chair that sat on the boardwalk fronting the hotel when the stage came rolling up with rivulets of dust cascading from the wheels, the leaders of the four-horse team high stepping until they came to a stop right in front of the hotel. Sam watched as the coach door swung open and out stepped a suited man who held his hand to help out an auburn haired lady. Another man in a suit got down behind her; the two men tipped their hats to the lady then walked away. She stood with a straight back while holding a parasol with one hand and her purse in the other while staring up and down the street as if she was looking for someone, or something, familiar. The sight of the woman intrigued him. She was young, pretty, shapely and neatly dressed like a lady of fine upbringing. Soon the stage driver opened the rear boot and set a rather large suitcase upon the boardwalk. The man tipped his hat to her then hopped aboard the stage and urged the team away with a 'yup, yup'. Sam figured the suitcase was too much for the woman to handle so he got out of his chair and walked over to see if she needed help. A good-looking woman, such as she, could get about any man to do it for her without even asking. It was a matter of who got there first.

'May I help you with your luggage, ma'am?' Sam asked.

The woman turned to face him, 'Why, yes, thank you. It is a bit heavy.'

Oh but she was lovely, he thought. Sam's heart rate had increased by just being near her. She had long auburn hair done up in curls atop her head, green eyes offset by a pale face which was very lightly freckled, ruby-red lips and an enchanting smile. She stood five foot six and was light of weight. The sight of her had reduced Sam to silence as he was not used to being so close to a lovely woman. She broke the stalemate when she said, 'Thank you for your help. I'm Ellen Riggs.'

'Sam, uh, Sam Hall, glad to help.' He got hold of the handle of the suitcase; hefted it, then began to walk into toward the hotel entrance.

'Oh no, wait, not in there!' she said.

Sam stopped in mid-stride and turned to face her.

'There, over there.' She pointed down the street.

The only building down the street where she was pointing, was the Scarlet Rose Saloon. At first Sam was in disbelief. One would not think that a lady this finely dressed had dealings with a saloon. If you found a woman in such a drinking establishment, she was usually a barmaid or a whore. Decent women didn't frequent such places, but who was he to argue?

'I'm to meet Mr Albert Wynn at the Scarlet Rose. He will see to my quarters,' she said. Puzzled, Sam led the way without comment into the saloon. There were only two customers sitting at a table. The bartender directed Sam and Ellen to a back office, presumed to be Wynn's. Sam set the suitcase down in front of the desk.

A short fat man came in from another room. 'Ellen! Come in, come in,' he said, then turned to face Sam as if to question his presence.

Ellen Riggs touched Sam's arm. 'Thanks again for your help Sam, maybe I'll see you later.'

Sam walked back into the saloon and when he asked the bartender about her, he told him, 'She's a new hire, I think. Albert said he met a fine one in St Louis and must have talked her into coming out here. She's a real looker, I'll say that much.' If the Scarlet Rose was to employ a lady of such striking appearance then Sam wanted to get to know her before she was subjected to the rough nature of cattle town saloons. He left, figuring to return later.

Sam spent the remainder of the afternoon buying a new suit of clothes and a new Stetson. He put it on, looked at himself in a mirror then dropped his old sweat-stained hat in a trash bin. Later he busied getting a shave and generally cleaning himself up with the intent to see Ellen Riggs again. It was mid-evening, after supper had been eaten and lamps lighted in the growing darkness, when Sam took a table seat in the Scarlet Rose. The saloon had a room-length bar with a brass foot rail against one wall. Four of a dozen tables before the bar were occupied by various gamblers busily swishing cards or calling for bets while seated patrons worried their chips in apprehensive hands. Four other tables were taken by groups of three or four men, busily gabbing about cattle, horses, whiskey and women. Two loudly dressed women walked about laughing and talking to one man then another, occasionally slipping a hand to a shoulder.

Sam kept watch to see if Ellen Riggs would appear. A tall man in a black suit walked up to the table and placed a glass of beer in front of him. Sam looked up. It was the young man who had taken over the lines of the runaway wagon yesterday. 'I never got your name but I want to thank you again for stopping that team,' the man said.

Sam stood and stuck out his hand. 'Sam Hall.'

'Wyatt Earp, Deputy Marshal of Wichita.'

Sam held out his hand toward a chair. 'Thanks for the drink, Marshal. Can I buy you one in return?'

'No thanks, Sam, I'm on duty, but I will sit a spell. I didn't hardly recognize you with all those fine clothes you have on.'

Sam smiled. 'My trail clothes were getting a little threadbare. Besides I wanted to look decent when the new lady in town comes out; Miss Riggs, she just came in on the stage today.'

Wyatt smiled. 'I heard that Wynn was bringing in a new girl. I guess I'd like to see her myself. Other than a pretty face what brings you to Wichita, Sam?'

'Oh I'm just footloose right now; I just finished a drive to Ellsworth and I'm making my way back to Texas.'

'You've done well with your earnings: many of the hands who finish up here usually spend most of their money on liquor and gambling in one night on the town.'

Their conversation was suddenly interrupted when someone began yelling, 'Get out! You son-of-bitch, this ain't the outhouse!' It was the bartender. He stood behind the bar and was swinging an axe handle over the bar at a grinning cowboy standing a few feet away. The drunken cowboy swayed back and forth on his feet as he pissed on the front of the bar. The inebriated cowboy moved his head out of the way whenever the axe handle came swishing by and continued to urinate. 'Yee haw!' he yelled 'This whole place is an outhouse!'

Earp jumped to his feet and hastened over. He drew his six-gun, then, using the butt, swung a hit to the back of the drunken cowboy's head. The man crumpled into his own puddle. Wyatt stood over the unconscious man. 'Who's with this man?' he called out, while looking over the hushed crowd.

A man in rumpled trail garb stepped forward. 'We were playing cards. We'd both been losing a lot, when he was all in, on that last hand. He said he was going to the outhouse.

I thought he meant he was going outside. If I'd known what he was up to I'd have stopped him for sure, but I was still in the game,' the man said. 'He usually don't cause any trouble; he just caint handle the whiskey.'

'That's pretty obvious,' Earp said.

'I'll get him out of here and to his room, Marshal; that's if you'll let me. He won't be no more trouble.'

Wyatt steadied a gaze at the man, 'He's going to jail! The best thing you can do is to get a mop and bucket and clean this mess up; it would be to your partner's benefit when he faces the judge tomorrow.'

'I'll take care of it, Marshal,' the man said, then began reaching to get his partner off the floor. Wyatt accompanied the two men, lending a hand to steady the drunken cowboy as they walked.

Sam settled back into his chair to await the arrival of Ellen Riggs.

Two hours and three glasses of beer later Sam was getting tired of waiting as Ellen had still not appeared. Perhaps she wouldn't show at all, having made the stage ride and it being the first day. Maybe she took the evening off, he surmised.

A pudgy brunette with excessive paint walked up and stood beside Sam's chair and began rubbing his neck. 'You look a little lonely sitting here drinking on your own,' she said.

'I'm waiting to see if Ellen Riggs is ever going to come out,' Sam replied.

'The new girl? Oh yes, everyone is asking about her. Her door is closed,' the woman said, then sat herself in a chair next to Sam. 'Why don't you buy a girl a drink and talk to me for a while? I'm new here, too. I've been away in St Louis for the past couple of weeks. I just got in town yesterday. Why, I'm practically a virgin.'

Sam grinned. 'Go ahead and order yourself a drink if you want, but I'm still waiting on Ellen.'

The woman stood abruptly. 'To hell with you! I ain't playing second fiddle to anybody! You might be waiting all night. I heard that the princess won't even show until tomorrow,' she said sardonically, then turned and left.

Sam was surprised by the woman's words but figured a bit of womanly jealousy was bound to happen. A lady like Ellen Riggs was probably tired from her trip. Before waiting all night for her, he'd walk back to Wynn's office and ask about Ellen, but first, after all that beer, he needed to take a leak. Just as he stood, he heard a 'pop' that sounded like a slap to someone's face. He turned in time to hear a yelp of pain and saw a skinny saloon girl in a gaudy red dress hit the floor face down. A tall man in new clothes stood over her. 'That bastard!' someone said loudly. A dozen men standing at the bar turned to see the scuffle. Tables of patrons stopped their gaming to stare silently.

The girl on the floor rolled to her back and kicked out at the man who stood and reached for her. 'Leave me alone, you son of a bitch!'

The man grabbed her by a shoulder and dragged her upright. He back-handed her, the force of which sent her to the floor again.

The girl's eyes were wide with fright. Sam thought he could read an anxious pleading in her look. He did not want a physical confrontation with this man or any other man and then be subject to the consequences that would be sure to result. He looked at the anxiety in those eyes and forced his caution aside, if nothing else for the girl's sake. He would not just stand by and allow this any longer.

Sam's expression suddenly became grim. He walked a few steps toward the scuffle and held his left hand palm out in a peace-making move.

'Whoa, hold on there a minute, mister, there's no need to rough the little lady up!' All eyes turned to look at Sam, including those of the man who was an inch or so taller than Sam and outweighted him by thirty pounds or so.

He glared at Sam. 'This ain't any of your damned business! You piss ant!' He starred at Sam for a moment then stepped forward and kicked at the girl on the floor as she attempted to get up.

'That's enough! You hear?' Sam ordered gruffly. The man looked to Sam with a murderous stare. 'Move on, or I'm apt to stomp your ass!'

Sam stepped forward to stand right in front of him. The saloon remained silent as if holding a breath, waiting to see what would happen next.

The man threw a haymaker in Sam's direction and he dodged the wild swing. Sam had learned long ago from an old fighter to throw his punch from where his fist was rather than draw back and telegraph your intention. He threw a straightforward eighteen-inch punch into the man's bulging stomach. The man doubled over with pain and the loss of his air, but only momentarily. He attempted another wild swing at Sam, only to be met by a thunderous right directed at the man's jaw. The man fell over a table; breaking the legs off it and crashing it to the floor. He lay still and sucked air heavily.

Deputy Marshal Earp suddenly appeared to stand before Sam. 'I turn my back for a minute and things get out of hand. You mind telling me what went on here?'

A man standing nearby answered for Sam. 'That big guy was beating up on Marla; knocked her to the floor twice. This fella stepped in and put a stop to it; just like we all would have done, Marshal, if it had gone on any longer.' Sam eyed the man disbelievingly.

'Where's Marla?' Earp asked.

'Right here, Marshal,' Marla answered. She was standing next to the bar dabbing a wet bar towel to her face. 'That bastard got mad because I wouldn't do things to him while sitting at his table. Unspeakable things that are done in private! That man stopped him. He's a good one!'

The marshal turned back to look at Sam. 'Well now, I usually arrest those who disturb the peace, but it appears you did nothing more than attempt to preserve it. There is, however, some damage done.' He looked over to the bartender. 'What do you think, Mason?'

Mason Call stepped around in front and looked at the damage. 'Looks like a table and a chair was busted up,' he said.

'Twenty dollars cover it?' Sam asked.

The bartender nodded his head up and down. 'Yeah, sure, that would be more than fair.'

Sam produced his wallet, opened it and extracted a large stack. The eyes of the saloon watched as he counted out twenty dollars in small bills then replaced the rest into the wallet and into his coat pocket. 'What about him?' Sam asked while motioning his head to the man on the floor.

'Oh, he's going to jail for the night. He'll see the judge tomorrow. He'll get a fine and be told to leave town,' Earp said.

Two men helped the marshal get the fallen man up and out the door. Sam watched them leave then turned to Mason who was behind the bar. 'You do have an outhouse, don't you?'

'Straight back from the door.' Mason pointed to a door near the end of the bar. 'There's a lantern hanging on the outside wall. Take it with you, if you want.'

Sam nodded then walked through the back door, took hold of the lantern and went on to the outhouse.

When finished with his business, Sam opened the door and stepped out with the lantern held in one hand. The spring-held door slapped shut. 'Don't make a move!' A voice from the darkness advised. Sam did not move. 'Set the lantern down, then hands up!' the voice commanded. Presuming that a gun was being held on him, Sam complied. He stood still as a hand from the shadows took his six-gun out of his holster then reached into his coat pocket and took his wallet. A second voice asked, 'Did you get it?'

'Yeah, I got it,' the first voice confirmed. Sam stood perfectly still then someone hit him over the head with a hard object and everything went black.

When Sam woke up he was lying down, not on the hard ground behind the saloon but on a bunk. He turned his head to look around and saw the bars. He was in jail but the cell door was open. Daylight showed through the barred window in the cell. He wondered how he had gotten here; his brain fogged straining for a memory.

'Ah, you're awake,' a familiar voice said. It was Deputy Marshal Earp.

Sam tried to rise. He faltered then lay back down.

'Take it easy,' Earp said, 'I'll get you something to drink.' He left the room then came back in with a steaming coffee cup. 'This will help clear your head.' With one hand he lifted up Sam's head and placed the coffee cup to Sam's lips with the other. Sam took a sip of the coffee laced with rye whiskey. Sam nodded his thanks. Earp set the cup on a nearby chair.

'Take some more when you want,' Earp said. Sam lay for a minute then slowly raised himself up and swung around to sit on the bunk. He reached over and took the cup, gulping a generous amount. 'Thanks,' Sam said. Earp nodded.

'How did I get here?' Sam asked.

'I had you brought over last night,' Wyatt said, 'for your own protection. It wasn't long after I took that other fellow to jail that I was summoned to the back of the Scarlet Rose. That's where you were found lying in front of the outhouse. I know that you were robbed, I'd just like to hear your side of it.'

'Right after you left, I went out to relieve myself. When I stepped out of the outhouse, two men took my new gun and my wallet then knocked me out. That's all that I know.'

'Did you see them?'

'No, they remained in the shadows.'

'How do you know there were two of them?'

Sam told of hearing two different voices. 'I realize that I made a big mistake showing the contents of my wallet

53

inside the saloon for all to see. Now I guess I'm broke again,' he lamented.

'Not quite!' Earp beamed. 'After you were safely lodged here, I went back to the Scarlet Rose and talked to Mason, the bartender. He described two men who had been there all evening drinking and gambling; apparently losing in their efforts for one of them had asked Mason for two dollars in exchange for his six-gun so he could continue the game. Mason gave him the two dollars then that fracas between you and that other fella began.

'Mason remembered the two leaving about the time you did, but they did not come back again. They most likely were standing at the bar watching when you paid Mason for the damages. When you left to go out back they did too. The only cover they provided was that they went out the front door instead of the back and quickly doubled around back to greet you when you stepped out.'

'Did you find them?' Sam inquired.

'I did,' Wyatt said, 'two doors down at the Golden Horn. I located them by Mason's description. They were involved in a card game and freely buying drinks for the table and three of the girls who work there. Oh, they were having a grand ol' time of it laughing and spending your money. Of course, they told me they had won the money earlier while gambling at the Scarlet Rose. I took a little over four hundred off them. You'll get it back after I explain things to Judge Castle. One of them had a brand new Colt in his holster. Funny thing was that the new Colt was a .45 calibre while all the cartridges in his belt were for a .44. Jock Avery, the gunsmith, confirmed the serial number was the one he sold to you. I've got it for you when you are ready.'

Sam rested in the cell and was awake when Wyatt herded the two prisoners out to the courthouse. He left before they returned, making his way to his hotel room to clean up and change clothes. Sam had a few loose dollars in his pockets so he went to the hotel restaurant for a meal. He was supping coffee when Wyatt walked in and stood beside his table. 'I figured you would be here.' He handed an envelope to Sam. 'They confessed so here's what's left of your money.'

Sam took the envelope. 'Thanks, Wyatt, I didn't think I would ever see that again.'

Wyatt also handed him his .45 Colt. 'I believe this is yours.' Sam smiled and took the six-gun. He wasn't wearing his holster so he laid the firearm on the table.

'Join me for some food, Wyatt?'

Wyatt reached into his coat pocket and produced a folded newspaper which he dropped in front of Sam, then took a chair. 'Are you that Sam Hall?' he asked.

Sam was taken aback, wondering what Wyatt was talking about. Wyatt pointed to the newsprint, a copy of *The Wichita Tribune*. BOUNTY HUNTER NABS J.D. SELDON,' was the headline on the second page. Sam looked at the article borrowed from the *Ellsworth Reporter*. He read: 'Bounty hunter Sam Hall caught up with the notorious outlaw J.D. Seldon Thursday night in the Golden Bull saloon. After a scuffle and a shootout, Seldon was shot dead along with a confederate as well as a companion of Hall's. Sheriff John Sikes said a $500 reward was paid to Hall who has since left Ellsworth.'

Sam looked up into the inquisitive stare of Wyatt Earp.

'That's me all right, only the story is a little flawed. I didn't shoot Seldon; he shot himself.' Sam could see by Wyatt's expression that he needed to say more so he told the whole story from the time he sat down at the card game with J.D. Seldon until he left Ellsworth. 'And that's how I got the money and that's how I come to be in Wichita,' Sam finished.

Wyatt sat quietly and seemed to be in deep thought, then he leaned toward the table. 'You seem to be a decent enough guy, willing to help out whether it be stopping runaway horses or coming to the aid of a whore. But that newspaper article has branded you as a man hunter and a killer. I haven't seen you shoot so I can't say if you're fast or accurate. I do know though, that a man faces certain responsibilities when he becomes deadly fast with a gun. Just like J.D. Seldon found out, you don't have to be the fastest gun when an unusual circumstance comes about. You just have to be lucky. It appears to me that you have a knack for getting into one scrape after another, but you've been lucky enough to come out pretty much unscathed, except for last night. That may not be the case if a man who lives by a fast gun takes a notion to test you.'

Sam looked at Wyatt when he finished talking. 'You are the second lawman who has said that I should go home and put this behind me. If you're saying that I should leave town, that is not a problem Wyatt, I just came here to rest up a bit as it is.'

'No need to think that I'm asking you to leave, because I'm not,' Wyatt said. 'I was just making a comment on what has happened to you in the last couple of days, that's all. I admire a man who won't just stand by and let bad things happen to someone who isn't capable of protecting themselves. You're doing for free exactly what I get paid to do in keeping the peace.'

Sam grinned. 'I wasn't looking for trouble with anyone. My experiences away from home are limited to cow camps, horse corrals and the trails. I'm a drover; never had any inclination to do much of anything else. I'm a little tired of trailing cattle right now, but unless opportunity presents a better way to make a living, I'll most likely be on another drive come springtime.'

Wyatt studied the young cowboy for a moment. 'Since you've been branded, I'd say you need to be on the lookout for those who might see fit to come after you. I've heard of that Seldon bunch before, although I've never met them, but I've only been here since my hiring in April. Others say Ben or some of his men come to town from time to time, usually after a few head of cattle are delivered. Of course, you knew that J.D. was a killer; at least that is what you got paid the bounty for. His brother Ben lives on a spread down in Cherokee County near Baxter Springs. It's over a hundred miles to Baxter Springs, a fair distance, south-east of here, a few miles from the Missouri border and a couple of miles from the Indian Territory. It's a perfect place for what Ben Seldon has going there.

'It's been said that Ben raids any passing cattle herds that come up the Shawnee Trail and manages to sneak off enough to keep him and his bunch in tobacco and whiskey while they do other things, like robbing out-of-the-way places, or vulnerable travelers, particularly those travelling alone. Let's say for the sake of speculation that the fellow who shot your friend rode out of Ellsworth and went straight to Seldon's place—'

Sam cut in, 'And if he didn't go back but just rode away?'

Wyatt pointed to the newspaper. 'Well, it's not exactly a secret any longer. Let's assume that Ben Seldon can read as well as you and I can. The point is that neither of us knows Ben Seldon or if he has intentions to avenge his brother's death. If not already, it will be only a matter of time, a few days at the most, until Ben Seldon knows; then the question is, will he do something about it?'

Sam sat quietly. 'I understand, but no one knows that I'm here, in Wichita.'

Wyatt was quick to answer. 'There are no secrets around here. Seldon and his bunch stay at a hotel when they come to town; might be the one you're staying at. The steak you had for supper last night most likely came from a steer that was delivered by Seldon. People talk; it won't be long before the whole town will know who Sam Hall is and that he is right here in Wichita.'

CHAPTER 9

When the shack that Ben Seldon called his ranch house, came into view, Leroy Hagen stopped his horse and sat looking at the structure while he nervously rolled a smoke. Though he had been on the trail for two days, he was in no hurry to face Ben. He was still unsure of what reaction he would get when he told him about J.D. Leroy finished his cigarette, then, with a gloved hand he squeezed the fire out of the butt and took up his reins. He was resolved to get the distasteful task over so he kneed his horse forward. Three saddled horses lazed at a hitch rail in front of the building. Leroy nosed his horse next to the others. No one came out of the shack. He tied his reins then clomped up the stairs to the porch.

When he opened the door he could see the bulk of Ben Seldon lounging in a chair next to a potbellied stove. Seldon was a big man, six feet tall and weighing over 200 pounds. He had a ruddy complexion, thin, dark hair that surrounded a fat face and pig-like eyes. Three others sat around in scattered chairs. Leroy glanced at them, recognizing each man as his eyes swept the room.

' 'Bout time you showed your sorry ass up here!' Ben boomed.

'I got here, quick as I could,' Leroy offered.

Ben grimaced. 'Hell, I know how long it takes to ride from Ellsworth to here. You stopped off for a spell someplace; can't keep your hands off a jug, I expect.'

'I stopped in Newton to rest my horse, then two days of riding to get here. It's better than a hundred miles from here to Newton,' Leroy said.

Ben spat a stream of tobacco juice into a can next to his chair, 'No matter, I already know about J.D. All I need from you are the particulars!'

Leroy was relieved that Ben hadn't gone into a tirade but he was still wary of what he might do. He did his best to tell of the night's events in Ellsworth. 'Larry and I were still in a game, J.D. was in another. We didn't know nothing was going on until J.D. started yelling about being cheated. It wasn't long before he was scuffling with a fella and then a shot was fired. Next thing I saw was J.D. lying on the floor. We checked him out but he was done for. There was two of 'em standing there; it looked to me like they were daring us to step in. Larry wasn't going to let J.D.'s shooting go unheeded, so, when he drew on 'em, I did too. I don't know who was the faster, them or us, but Larry and I both got off shots. Larry went down and I know that the one I shot went down too.'

'Why didn't you shoot the other one?' Ben sneered.

Leroy gulped. 'I thought Larry had shot him. It happened so quick, I didn't know what the bartender was going to do with that scattergun, so I got the hell outa there!'

Ben Seldon nodded his head in understanding. 'I reckon I'd have been ready to leave myself, but I might've thrown a bit more lead.'

Leroy breathed a sigh of relief.

'You reckon that you could recognize the one who was still standing?' Ben asked.

'I didn't get much of a look,' Leroy stammered. 'Tall, medium build, sandy hair. He looked like just another cattle drover to me.'

Ben glared at him. 'Bah, and you've described about half the drovers between here and Texas! Try and think, Leroy. Did he have any scars or marks on him? What kind of gun was he shooting?'

Leroy thought for a moment. 'No, nothing out of the ordinary. I didn't see his gun, but I expect I could recognize him again if I was to see him.'

'Fine, fine,' Ben said. 'We know his name and that he left Ellsworth the next day after he collected the reward on J.D. Word is that he rode out alone. We just gotta figure out where he went to, that's all!

'I'm putting out a reward on his head. A thousand dollars; twice what he collected on J.D.'

Leroy stood looking at Ben in questioning manner. Ben noticed the look. 'J.D. and I might have not seen eye to eye on some things but still, he was my kin. I caint let this fella get away with shooting J.D. and get paid to do it! I expect J.D. would have done the same for me.'

Ben turned to the men seated about, directing his attention to Wink Robbins, the closest to him. Tall and rangy, Wink Robbins, whose real name was John, was so called because he had a tic to his right eye that caused his eye to blink uncontrollably. Wink was not especially fast with a gun but he was ruthless and wouldn't hesitate to shoot someone at the slightest provocation. The blinking of his eye while facing an opponent appeared comical, as if he was frightened; that he could be easily taken. The last smiling drunk became so mesmerized by the man's blinking eye, when he should have been watching Wink's hand hovering over his six-gun, that it cost him his life. When the man turned, grinning, and smirked to a friend nearby, Wink drew his Colt and sent a slug right in the center of his breastbone.

'Wink,' Ben began, 'you go up to Abilene; nose around; see if our man went there. Those who come to this country tend to hang out at familiar places. I'm thinking that this cowboy has been to Abilene or some such place before and will head there to spend some of that money. But, if you get the word out to others about the reward, we might just catch him. If you happen to locate that bastard either shoot him or just come and get me. I wouldn't mind sending some lead his way!' Then he looked to Charlie Roades, a man whose clothes always looked rumpled like he slept in them. At five foot ten, and 150 pounds, he was not an imposing figure, but he was wiry and known to have nerve. And Reg Moss, who stood at five foot three and looked beefy. Reg was known for opening his mouth either to complain of having to do some chore, or to compliment himself while drinking, which he was prone to do in excess. 'You two check out Newton, Wichita and Caldwell. Spread the word to those you know and to our customers. A thousand dollars to the man who brings him to me.'

'Ben, can I trade with Wink?' Reg Moss asked. 'I figure that marshal in Wichita ain't forgotten about me busting up that saloon. There might even be a dodger out on me.'

Ben's mouth flew open. 'A dodger!' he exclaimed. 'For what, being a loud mouth drunk and getting into a scrape? They only put dodgers out on robbers and killers who get careless. You keep at it though and there is going to be one out on you for sure. No! No swapping, Wink don't need any help; he works better by himself. If you don't learn to quit trying to be tougher than you actually are when you get a little whiskey in you, Reg, then I expect you're going to run out of saloons and towns to do your drinking in!' The others snickered. 'It's interfering with your work!'

Reg sheepishly dropped his eyes to the floor. 'I'll watch myself,' he said.

'See that you do!' Ben thundered. 'Maybe Charlie can keep a short rope on you until you get this job done!'

Ben waved a folded newspaper in the air. 'Get yourselves one of these newspapers; show it around to some of your kind in the saloons; then tell 'em about the reward I'm offering. That'll get a score of 'em out looking the country over!'

'How long you want us to stay out spreading the word?' Wink Robbins asked.

Ben thought for a moment. 'This is Monday, I reckon.' He moved his figures as he counted. 'I figure you can go wherever, spread the word, get your mouthing and drinkin' done, and be back here no later than Saturday night.'

'What if Reg and I end up killing this Sam Hall?' Charlie Roades asked.

'I hope you do!' Ben beamed. 'But whoever gets him has gotta bring his carcass here so that Leroy can identify him. No body, no reward.'

'What about some money, Ben?' Reg Moss asked. 'You know, some travelling money. Maybe a little extra so's we can get a drink later on; it don't have to be much.'

Ben's expression was amazed. 'By damn, I send you out on an errand and all you can think about is likker money?' He stood, then went to a saddle-bag and took out some coins. He handed each man a twenty-dollar gold piece. 'Take care of your horse and get some trail food. You go spending that on likker and whores, you'll starve before you get any more outa me!'

Leroy looked to Ben. 'What do you want me to do, Ben?'

'You just sit tight, Leroy, until this man is caught. You just stick with me like I was your kin. When we find out where Hall has gone to, you'll be going along to make the identification. For now though, you and I will be spreading the word around in Baxter Springs and on over to Joplin, in case he tries to give us the slip in Missouri.'

After Reg Moss and Charlie Roades had ridden off, Ben walked over to where Wink Robbins was saddling his horse. 'After you check out Abilene, Wink, drop on down to Newton and Wichita; check and see if those two do anything but drink. Charlie's OK but he can easily be led by anyone, including Reg Moss. I don't trust Reg; he ain't got a lick of sense and when he's out of my sight he's always pulling something stupid.'

Wink nodded his head. 'I'll see you Saturday.'

CHAPTER 10

Sam lounged around after Wyatt had left the restaurant, then went to his room to freshen up and rest. He lay on the bed contemplating sleep when he remembered Ellen Riggs. With all the disruptive events of last night there was no way of knowing if she ever came on to the floor of the saloon. He would find out tonight, for he surely did want to see her again. Sam slept soundly all afternoon long. About 6 p.m. he had a thick steak and mashed potatoes drowned in gravy. He figured on walking off the big meal so he headed to the livery to check on his horse. The animal looked to be in good shape and had been well fed. The night hostler's name was Felix, a thin man whose skin coloring suggested jaundice.

'I'd be happy to pay my bill to date,' Sam offered.

Felix looked to the floor, then raised his head. 'Are you staying in town for the night?' He asked.

Sam nodded. 'I'll most likely be around for a few days yet.'

Felix reached out and stroked the horse's withers. 'It would be better if'n you was to pay the boss man in the morning. That way I don't have to do any paperwork.' He paused for a moment. 'I ain't too good at figures and such.'

Sam smiled and put a hand to Felix's shoulder, 'That's not a problem, my friend. You take good care of my horse and I'll be grateful.' Sam stuck a dollar coin into Felix's pocket then gave the small man a friendly slap on the shoulder and walked away.

When Sam entered the Scarlet Rose he glanced around. The place was fairly busy with eight or ten men standing at the bar gabbing. Half-a-dozen tables were filled with drinkers and three card tables were busy. Sam stood at the end of the bar until Mason came to take his order.

Mason stuck out his hand. Sam took it and shook. 'I'm glad to see you,' Mason said. 'Sure sorry you got roughed up last night but it looks like you came out of it OK.'

'I did,' Sam said, 'thanks to Marshal Earp.'

'He's a good man,' Mason said. 'Now, what can I get for you, Sam?'

Sam stuck up two fingers. 'Two things, Mason, one cold beer and then information on Ellen Riggs.'

Mason smiled, his eyes sweeping over to the card tables. 'She's dealing on table number three.'

Sam was both surprised and elated to see that Ellen wasn't one of the regular girls. 'I'd've been in earlier if I'd known that. I had no idea she was a gambler.'

Mason smiled, then set a mug of beer in front of Sam. 'No one knew except her and Albert Wynn. He just spread the word that a new girl was coming. Al's always coming up with ways to increase business and this one is working fine.

She has a waiting line to get to her table.'

'How do I get in line?' Sam asked.

'I'll put your name down,' Mason said, 'I figure it will be a couple hours. No one's lasting very long, but they ain't complaining about it.'

It was near midnight when Mason came over to Sam. 'Fella just left the table, Sam, you're next.'

Sam nodded his thanks then walked over to the table. Four chairs were filled by other gamblers. The one empty chair was immediately to Ellen's left. Sam slipped on to the seat.

'The game is Twenty-one. It costs a dollar to play with a five-dollar limit on bets. Dealer hits on sixteen,' Ellen said, in a practiced announcement to all new players. She had been looking at the cards and the table when Sam seated himself. When she looked up, a smile of recognition greeted him.

'Oh, hello, Sam,' She chirped.

Sam was made speechless by her musical voice, sweet, smiling face, good white teeth and soft locks of shiny auburn hair done up in a pile on top of her head. She had been a pretty girl when just a youngster, he figured; now she had grown into a beautiful woman with no toll taken on the years between girlhood and womanhood. Sam understood why no one was winning at her table but her. The men were just as enchanted by her as he was, so they made foolish bets without thinking while she smiled and whisked the cards around the table, calling each one as it landed in a gambler's pile. Ultimately, each bettor left after depositing what money he had gambled. There were no threats or heated exchanges with the dealer. The losers left smiling.

After half-a-dozen hands had been played, Sam had won two and a round-bellied fellow across the table had taken another, the rest were taken by Ellen Riggs. She placed the deck on the table. 'Gentlemen, it's time for us all to take a little break; stretch your legs a little and refresh your drinks.' She stood and looked at Sam. 'Would you escort me to the bar, Sam?'

Sam stood. Ellen looped her arm into his and they walked to the end of the bar. Mason was standing there when they walked up. 'Just a glass of water, Mason,' Ellen said. Sam put his empty beer mug on the bar for a refill.

'I almost did not recognize you, Sam, when you first sat down. You've changed for the better; all cleaned up and with new clothes,' Ellen said. 'I heard that you came to Marla's rescue last night, then later on became a victim yourself. I'm pleased that you appear to be all in one piece.'

Sam nodded. 'Marshal Earp not only caught the culprits but was able to retrieve most of my money too. Otherwise, I'd be looking around for a loan.'

Ellen smiled. 'Let me know if you ever need one. As you can see, I'm not just one of the saloon girls. I'm here just for the gambling. It's how I make my living and I usually have a few dollars to spare for a friend.'

Sam's heart fluttered when she had called him a friend. 'Thank you, Ellen, I was hoping we could be friends.'

'We are, Sam. I would like to see more of you and not just from across a card table.'

'You don't want me to play cards with you?'

Ellen grinned. 'If you want to play just for fun, by all

means sit in, but I must warn you that I am a professional gambler and eventually I will beat you.'

'Would you be interested in breakfast tomorrow?' Sam asked.

She nodded. 'As long as it isn't too early. I'm a working girl who keeps long hours.'

'Say ten o'clock at the hotel restaurant.'

'I'll be there, Sam, I wouldn't miss it,' she said, then turned and walked back to the gaming table.

CHAPTER 11

Reg Moss and Charlie Roades had ridden to Newton, arriving late in the afternoon. Prior to July 1871 the Newton prairies were devoid of inhabited dwellings, but when the AT & SF railroad ran a line through the area, a proposed stop was made. Newton began as a collection of tents and shacks sited near the tracks a mile and a half from the stockyards being built at the time. Within three months there was a population of over 500. Now three years later, Newton was like any other end-of-the-line cattle town, wild, raucous and roaring during the cattle shipping season, quiet during the off season when the card sharks, whores and petty thieves left town for their wintering grounds in St Louis or other points east.

Newton was quiet now, not because the season was over, but because the railroad had extended its line south from Newton to Wichita. The numerous creeks and sixty miles of good grazing land just south of Wichita made for a better holding ground for arriving herds. So the business shifted to Wichita and most of the herd owners were now selling their cattle there. It was only twenty-five miles that separated Newton from Wichita, but that saved the herders two days of trail travel.

Reg Moss and Charlie Roades had already conferred during their day-long ride and decided that they wanted that reward money for themselves. Oh, they would go through the motions of telling a few about it; saying that the last they heard was that Sam Hall was headed back to where he came from in Texas, that he was riding alone and was avoiding any settlements. That would put a few, quick money hopefuls on the open trails, freeing up the towns for Reg and Charlie to capitalize on, should they find Sam Hall on their own.

The two asked at the livery, mercantile and hotel, with no luck, before settling in to haunt the saloons. By evening the two had wandered to the seamier side of town known as Hide Park that sprouted numerous saloons in the middle of the red-light district. They sat at a table in the Red Horse Saloon gulping shots of rye whiskey followed by swigs of beer.

'He didn't come this way,' Charlie Roades said. 'Tomorrow, I guess we'll ride on down to Wichita and see if he showed up there.'

Reg Moss leaned back in his chair. 'What the hell's the hurry, Charlie? Ben said to spread the word around. He didn't say we had to be in a hurry about it. I got a hankering to catch that little blonde who just danced by here. I don't figure to feel up to riding very much in the morning.' Then he reached for a nearby bottle of whiskey.

The drink began to flow faster as the night lengthened, as did Reg Moss's mouth. A slim young man, by the name of Jay Bradford, blond of hair, dressed in new shirt, trousers and shiny boots had joined the duo at their table. He had a low slung .36 caliber cap and ball Navy Colt resting in a holster tied to his leg. Jay Bradford was cock-sure and looking to gain a reputation of his own. 'This Sam Hall must be pretty good with a six-gun,' Bradford mentioned, after Reg had shown him the newspaper article.

'Good enough that there's a thousand-dollar bounty on his head for shooting ol' J.D.!' Charlie beamed.

'So if someone should outdraw this guy, how does he go about collecting?' Jay asked.

'Just ride over to Baxter Springs and find Ben Seldon's place, everyone around there knows where Ben's is located. You'd have to take the body with you though; Ben won't pay up unless he sees it. You gotta have proof!' Reg lectured, then added, 'Me and Charlie aim to collect that reward soon as we catch up to Hall.'

'Where you figure he went to?' Jay asked.

Reg smiled broadly. 'We've been telling folks that he headed back to Texas.'

'That's pretty broad,' Jay stated. 'What do you really believe?'

Reg was feeling no pain and was slurring his words as he leaned close to Jay as if what he was going to say was a secret. 'I've been asking myself what I would do if I'd just collected a five-hundred-dollar reward.'

Charlie overheard. He leaned over the table and announced jovially, 'Hell, Reg, you'd go to the nearest saloon, get drunk, then blow a bunch in a whorehouse!'

Reg slapped his knee. 'That's exactly what I figure that Sam fella will do. Ol' Ben ain't so dumb sending us out to the towns to check them out. I figure that he knows that we are apt to find Hall in one of these dives, or at least locate where he's gone. Ben's testing us to see if this guy is any good, or just got lucky. And if we get bumped off, then Ben will know that he's on the right track. It pays to be smart, like me!'

'Anybody else know of this?' Jay asked.

'We just started in today. We'll be going down to Wichita tomorrow, or the next day, and then on down to Caldwell. We got a man who went up to Abilene to spread the word there and I expect Ben Seldon himself will be looking around Baxter Springs, Joplin and other places,' Reg advised.

Jay leaned back in his chair. 'Can I read that paper again?'

'Sure, sure, help yourself. Here, I'll buy you another drink.'

Jay took the extended paper and muttered, 'No thanks on the drink; I've got to get an early start in the morning.'

Jay was interested in finding Sam Hall himself, it was a plum worthy of the picking, but he didn't need these two yokels to get in his way. Once he took down Sam Hall, word would get out and he would be the top gun to beat. The reward would be icing on the cake. The fact that the offer was being blabbed all over meant that he would have to react quickly and get on the trail before someone else got to Hall before he did. He studied the paper; handed it back then left. As he walked to his hotel room he pondered whether to ride to Ellsworth and get all the info first hand and pick up the trail from there, or go ahead and get a jump on those two drunks and check out Wichita for himself. By the time he reached the hotel, he had figured to make the twenty-five mile ride to Wichita in the morning. If he left early he could be there by mid-morning while his two drinking friends were apt to be just getting up.

CHAPTER 12

Sam was fifteen minutes early for the pre-arranged breakfast meeting with Ellen Riggs. He asked the waitress for the furthest table in the back, insuring the most privacy. Sam took a chair with his back against the wall so that he could watch when Ellen came in. It was right at ten o'clock when Sam stood to greet her. He was flabbergasted again by her beauty. She wore a light-grey and white gingham dress; her shoulders were covered with a white shawl. It looked as if she had spent much time arranging her perfectly done hair curled atop, just like he had remembered at their first meeting. Height wise, she would easily fit under his chin except for the hair. She flashed a smile that warmed Sam all over. He pulled out a chair and seated her. 'Glad you could make it,' he said.

'I told you last night that I wouldn't miss it,' Ellen giggled.

They had a light meal and lots of coffee making small talk until Ellen said, 'Tell me about yourself, Sam, where do you come from and how did you come to be in Wichita?'

Sam did not feel the need to spill out everything to Ellen Riggs just yet. 'There isn't much to tell. I'm a born and bred Texan. I grew up on a small spread near Dallas. I tried my hand at a few things. I was a ranch hand for a neighbor for a time until I found out the pay was little more than food for the day. I signed on to help a fella freighting some implements. It paid pretty well but the job didn't last long. Young as I was at the time I was looking for something with a little more excitement to it so I signed on to trail herd cattle. I've never had the opportunity to do anything that required a lot of schooling, which I don't have, and as a consequence, I've spent most of my working life herding cattle down in Texas. I just finished up a drive to Ellsworth and am currently just footloose and will eventually, most likely, head on back to Texas and sign on to do another drive.'

Ellen smiled lightly. 'You're more than just a cattle drover, Sam. Like you say, you haven't had the opportunity to discover other means to make your way. Things like that just seem to come along naturally. If you like what you do then what is wrong with that?'

Sam put his elbows on the table and clasped his hands together. 'Not a thing. I like the cattle business and at some time I plan on getting a small herd started on a piece of ground of my own. Having just spent three months living with a bunch of mangy critters makes me rethink that from time to time. Right now I'm just trying to enjoy my off time and maybe look around a bit.'

'Which you deserve,' Ellen said. 'I can't imagine spending three months travelling and camping out. I guess I wouldn't make a very good pioneer.'

Sam flashed a warm smile. 'Looks like you don't have to. From what I observed last night you'll never go hungry, or have to look very far to find work. You had those card players eating out of your hand and not one gripe when they lost.'

Ellen smiled. 'I just try to make everyone feel comfortable,' she laughed.

'You do a good job of doing that,' Sam said. 'Now, what about you, how did you happen to come to Wichita?'

Ellen sat back in her chair. 'That's easy; the same as you, Sam, I came here out of circumstance. After some attending school in Philadelphia I returned to my family's home in St Louis where I met John Carpenter Riggs. He was a dashing man, handsome and well groomed. He swept me off my feet and we married. John's employment called for travel. He was a gambler by profession and very good at it: John was a riverboat gambling man. That's how we came to St Louis and where we made the acquaintance of Albert Wynn. John taught me how to gamble and win at numerous games. We made a pretty good team and did well for a while. Unfortunately, one day, John contracted cholera and soon after he was gone. Albert Wynn, whom John and I had met in St. Louis, knew of John's misfortune and offered an opportunity for me to come to Wichita and try my luck. He indicated it would be good for both of us.'

'I'm sorry for your loss,' Sam offered.

'Thank you, Sam,' Ellen said. 'It has been a time since John has been gone. I've learned to adjust, so here I am.'

Sam and Ellen whiled away the rest of the morning talking. The restaurant had filled up and a number of folks had finished their noon meal. It was after 1 p.m.

when Ellen said, 'It's been fun, Sam, and I'd like to see more of you, but now I need to rest a little before starting my evening's work.' The two stepped out of the door and on to the boardwalk. Sam intended to walk Ellen back to the Scarlet Rose where she had a private room on the second floor.

They had taken scarcely half-a-dozen steps when a call came from the middle of the street, 'Sam Hall!' Jay Bradford hailed.

Sam let go of Ellen's arm and looked to see who was talking to him. The young man standing in the street wasn't recognizable, at least Sam didn't recall ever having made his acquaintance. He turned to face the man. 'I don't recall knowing you,' Sam said warily.

'I reckon you don't know me now, but folks will by the time I'm through here. The name is Jay Bradford, that's if you need to know the name of the man who's better than you are. I'm calling you out, Hall!'

Sam turned and motioned for Ellen to move away, which she did, then he turned back to face the challenger. The young man was no more than eighteen or twenty years old. Even from a distance Sam could see the youthful face, even featured and untouched as yet by trouble or time; no lines or strain from toil or hardships from frontier living were apparent. He had blond hair, was slim of build and his clean, new appearing clothes indicated that he had wealthy relatives who took good care of him. He sure didn't look the part of a gun slick or a ruffian. Why, Sam had seen rookie drag drivers and remuda herders looking tougher on their first day of work.

The young man had a holster tied down to his thigh.

His hand hovered loosely by his side, near the butt of the six-gun.

Sam was careful to keep his own hand close to the butt of his own gun, 'I have no fight with you!' Sam declared. 'What do you want?'

'Let's just say that I'm here on J.D. Seldon's account. You collected a reward for gunning him down and now I'm going to collect a reward for out-gunning you!'

'Reward you say, for gunning me?' Sam said.

'Oh, you don't know about it, eh? J.D.'s brother Ben has offered a thousand dollars to the man who takes you, alive or dead!' He emphasized the latter.

Sam stared at Bradford, figuring the kid wasn't bluffing but he wasn't about to be cowed by him either. 'Is the reward worth dying for?' he asked.

'I know I can beat you!' Jay Bradford said confidently.

'Back off!' Sam said. 'I don't want to fight you!'

Bradford smiled lightly. 'Well, I ain't giving you a choice.' With that he went into a crouch and reached for his gun at the same time. Sam dived and rolled to his right. His shoulder touched the boardwalk before he came to a kneeling position while drawing his gun at the same time. Three shots could be heard by a discerning ear, but two were so close together that it would seem to be one with an immediate echo. The third shot was from a distance away. The bullet intended for Sam buried itself into a board on the building behind him.

Jay Bradford stood in the street with his mouth fully open and his eyes wide with disbelief. His hand had let the gun down when he took the bullet in his breastbone. He clutched his chest with his free hand then tried to raise his gun again to the kneeling Sam Hall. Sam didn't want to shoot the youth again, but he held his .45 ready in case Bradford pursued this any further. Jay Bradford took one step, then fell forward on his face, landing heavily to the street. His gun arm with the gun gripped tightly in his hand, ended up stretched out past his head as his legs jerked spasmodically then he lay still.

Sam stood and walked over to him and kicked the gun from the lifeless hand. He looked about to see if there were another, perhaps a friend of Bradford's, lurking around. When no one made themselves known, Sam slid his gun back into his holster.

A cluster of people had gathered on the boardwalk near Ellen. One man pushed another out of the way in order to get a better look. A path opened through them as Sam walked up the steps. 'It's Hall,' someone on the edge of crowd said. 'That's Sam Hall, the bounty hunter, the one we read about who took out J.D. Seldon.'

A murmur raced through the crowd. 'Hall . . . Sam Hall. . . .'

'Are you sure that's him?'

'It's him, all right. I heard the kid call him by name before Hall shot him. Let me tell you that Hall is one fast sum-bitch!'

The comments shot back and forth and the path to Ellen almost closed as people in the rear pushed forward for a better look. Men stopped talking as Sam approached and silently moved to one side or the other to make room for him. One man nodded cautiously. A woman standing nearby looked at him then averted her eyes. No one addressed him directly, seeming to regard him as an object rather than a man. Sam offered no explanation until he walked to where Ellen stood.

'He gave you no choice, Sam. I'm so sorry that he pushed you to do that!' Ellen assured him while reaching a hand to his arm. 'Dreadful, just dreadful,' she lamented.

'I didn't want to do it. I tried to avoid it.' Sam complained.

A beefy man in a black suit coat and wearing a badge walked hurriedly to the prone Jay Bradford. He kneeled by the body for a moment then picked up the six-gun nearby; stood and stuck the gun in his belt then his gaze narrowed to Sam on the boardwalk. He came straight over to stand in front of Sam. 'You just killed that kid!' It was a statement rather than a question, so Sam figured that he had seen what had transpired and wondered why the man had not tried to intervene.

'I had no choice,' Sam said quietly.

'I'm Mike Meagher, Marshal of Wichita. I saw it from a distance down the street. I fired once into the air to get both of your attentions to stop what you were doing, but the kid drew on you and both of you shot at about the same time that I did.'

A round man wearing a bowler hat stepped forward. 'This man tried to talk the kid out of it, Marshal, but he wouldn't listen. The kid said he was going to collect a bounty on him. That kid was full of piss and vinegar looking to make a name for hisself, but he found out that Hall was faster, I reckon.' The marshal nodded his understanding. 'Sounds like self-defense to me.' He gazed around the little group to see if anyone contested that determination. Everyone there, including Ellen, either nodded affirmative or said yes. 'The kid asked for it!' one man asserted. Meagher glared at him and nodded. A short man wearing a carpenter's apron walked up. 'Do you think I should get busy making a coffin?' he asked. Meagher nodded. 'Get someone to help you move the body to your shop, but don't do anything with him until I check his pockets for any money or papers.

'I'll need to see you in my office,' Marshal Meagher said to Sam, then stood waiting for Sam to walk with him.

Sam turned to Ellen. 'I'll see you later,' he said, then turned and walked away with Meagher.

At the jailhouse, Sam took a chair in front of the marshal's desk as Meagher sat down and took a paper and pen in hand. 'I need your name.'

'Sam Hall.'

'Ever see that fella before?' Meagher scribbled while waiting for an answer.

'No, can't say as I have. He said his name was Jay Bradford.'

'No sense beating around the bush here, Sam. Deputy Earp told me about you and how you stopped a runaway team, then stepped in and prevented that whore Marla from getting beat on. He told me about you being mugged night before last. Now you got a stranger calling you out in the middle of the day. One minute you're a Good Samaritan and the next you're pure poison. What goes on here?'

Before Sam could answer, the door opened and Wyatt Earp walked in. He nodded to Sam then drew up a ladder-back chair and sat nearby.

'It's like I told Wyatt before; I got into a saloon fight up in Ellsworth and a fella pulled a gun on me. We wrestled on the floor; the gun went off and he took the bullet instead of me. It was enough to kill him. I found out later that it was J.D. Seldon. Two of Seldon's friends pulled their guns on me and my friend. My friend shot one of them and got shot in return by the other one who then escaped. The sheriff paid me a reward that I wasn't even aware existed, then he ordered me to leave town.'

'And then you came to Wichita,' Meagher finished for him. 'Why didn't you get on down the trail, back to where you came from?'

Sam did not know the answer to that but said, 'Wyatt had already warned me that a relative or friend of Seldon might come after me. I wasn't running from anything. I guess that I just didn't believe that anyone would actually do it.'

Meagher sat back in his chair. 'Some folks kill others out of jealousy or by accident; most of the time though it is done by some scoundrel looking for a way to collect some easy money. A man on the boardwalk back there said the kid was looking to collect a bounty on you. What do you know about that?'

Sam shrugged. 'Only what I heard from the kid; that Ben Seldon has offered a thousand-dollar reward for catching or killing me! It didn't take long for the word to get out.'

Marshal Meagher nodded. 'That word just cost that kid's life and there's bound to be others looking to get a crack at you. You're starting to draw flies, Hall. We don't want that kind of element to come to town. I believe it would be in the best interest of Wichita if you left. Don't think that I'm singling you out, Sam, that's the policy for anyone who uses a gun in Wichita. In your case it means without delay. You could leave now that you've rested up a bit couldn't you, Hall?'

Sam looked at the marshal with a withdrawn expression and nodded slowly. 'Might I be permitted to say goodbye to someone and get my stuff from the hotel and pick up some supplies?'

'Wyatt here will just walk along with you while you're doing that, then. I don't want anybody standing in your way while you're still in town.'

'I don't need any protection, but it's up to him if he wants to come. It won't bother me.'

'No, it ain't up to him: it's up to me! So, if you'll get on with what you figure you need to do, he'll walk along with you.'

Sam shrugged, stood and turned away. People moved to the side as the two men walked toward the Scarlet Rose, their boots thumping on the boards.

'I just need to see Ellen Riggs for a minute, Wyatt,' Sam said, hoping the lawman would allow him some privacy. Wyatt remained silent as the two walked in through the batwings. Those standing at the bar turned to gape. Mason saw them approach and quickly came to stand before them. 'Sam here is leaving town and would like a word with Miss Riggs,' Wyatt explained. 'He won't be but a minute.'

Mason nodded. 'I can go and see if she'll come down. Albert doesn't allow anybody up the stairs but him or her.' When Wyatt nodded, Mason walked over and began climbing the stairs. It seemed a long time before Mason and Ellen Riggs came down. She walked over to stand before Sam. 'Mason said you're leaving town, Sam.'

Sam took her arm and walked her a few feet away toward the door; the most privacy that they were to get. Wyatt leaned his back on the bar, folded his arms and watched.

'Ellen, I've been ordered out of town by Marshal Meagher. He figures that I am a bad influence and that me just being here could cause more trouble. I guess that I can't disagree with that. I just wanted to tell you how sorry I am at your having to see that gunfight and to say that someday and somehow I want to see you again.'

'The feeling is mutual, Sam. I'd very much like to see you, too. Have you decided where you are going?'

'I expect that I'll head on back to Texas. Fort Worth or Dallas, I guess. I grew up around there. But that's not important right now, Ellen. I figure that you won't stay in Wichita forever. Where do you plan on going from here, back to St Louis?'

Ellen looked at Sam for moment. 'I haven't planned that far ahead, Sam. There is really nothing for me to go back to in St Louis. I'll bet that they have gaming saloons in Fort Worth and Dallas. I've never been there, but who knows?'

Wyatt stepped forward. 'It's time,' he said flatly, the first words he had spoken since leaving the marshal's office.

Ellen stepped close, then put her arms around Sam's neck drawing his face to hers. She kissed him fully on the lips then turned and walked away. Sam didn't have time to react as Wyatt touched Sam's elbow, indicating for him to move on.

The clerk was standing behind the counter of the hotel when Sam and Wyatt walked through the lobby. 'I'll be checking out as soon as I get my gear,' Sam said, in passing.

'Yes, sir, I'll get your bill ready.'

Wyatt followed Sam into his room. 'I hope you don't mind; I need to put my trail clothes on,' Sam said. Wyatt took a chair facing the window while Sam busied changing his clothes. He strapped on his gunbelt, quickly checking the loads. He ejected the one spent cartridge, putting the empty into his shirt pocket and filling the chamber with a new one. He holstered the gun then lifted his saddle-bags to his shoulder, picked up his saddle gun and said, 'I'm all set.'

They went down the stairs, and Sam paused to leave the key and pay three dollars, the balance of his bill to date. The clerk bobbed his head up and down thanking Sam and inviting him to return. Sam smiled and nodded then turned toward the mercantile, Wyatt walking slowly along beside him, occasionally turning and glancing along the boardwalk in both directions. People walking toward them stood aside, staring. There were quiet comments and mutters and Sam heard his name mentioned more than once.

Sam walked to one end of the mercantile counter and put down his saddle-bags, saddle gun and bedroll. The storekeeper walked up smiling broadly.

'I need some supplies,' Sam said, then began naming off the items he wanted. The clerk bustled back and forth stacking bags, cans and packages on the counter,

'Smoking tobacco?' he asked.

Sam nodded. 'Two bags, papers and lucifers.'

'Stocking up, are you, Mr Hall? We've got some nice dried apricots and firm potatoes, if you'd like?' the clerk questioned.

'I'll take a coupla pounds of the apricots and five pounds of the potatoes and that should do it.'

The clerk bobbed his head, produced a paper and began adding up the prices. 'It comes to eight dollars and fifteen cents, Mr Hall. Would you like to check the figures?'

Sam shook his head. Taking out his pocketbook he placed a ten-dollar bill on the counter.

The clerk made change then put the purchases in a gunny sack. Wyatt scooped up the sack as Sam stooped to retrieve his goods from in front of the counter.

'I guess that you are headed home,' Wyatt stated, as they walked toward the livery.

'I figure to head in that direction,' Sam said.

'That might be the first place they would look,' Wyatt warned. 'I heard that there was good opportunity in Arizona. You might do well to disappear from your usual habits; change your name; start a new life.'

'Well, if they are intent on tracking me then it most likely won't matter where I go,' Sam replied.

Felix had a stern expression on his face when Sam and Wyatt entered the livery. 'There was a young fella that come in early asking questions; said he was looking for you. I told him to check the hotel. Was that OK, Sam?'

Sam realized how easy it was for anyone to find him. 'He found me, Felix. I need to settle my bill and move on.'

'I'll get the boss man so's he can give you the numbers.'

Sam was muttering to himself as he trotted his horse out of town, 'Damn, another night on the trail.'

CHAPTER 13

Two hours after Sam had left, Reg Moss and Charlie Roades rode into Wichita, having left Newton with aching heads and little remaining cash. They had about twelve dollars between the two of them having squandered a good portion of the twenty dollars that Ben had given each man, on liquor, gambling and saloon girls. 'I need a drink,' Reg Moss said, guiding his horse to a hitch rack in front of a seedy saloon on the west side of Wichita.

'We ought to get a room and board these horses before we get to drinking, Reg,' Charlie Roades stated.

'We got all night!' Reg Moss declared, then slipped out of his saddle and headed to the saloon entrance.

By the time the two were working on their second nickel beer they had learned all the events of the earlier part of the day. Sam Hall had been here, had killed another man in a fast draw, just this very afternoon, and had left town, heading to Texas; not long ago, the word was.

'We can get on his trail, if we take off right now,' Charlie Roades insisted.

Reg Moss was in no mood to leave what comforts he had. 'Morning will be soon enough; we got to rest them horses,' he said, then turned back to his drink.

Charlie Roades would have no part of sitting idle after they had done just that for the past two nights. Now that they had a hot lead on Sam Hall's whereabouts, Roades wanted to go after him. 'We want that reward we got to get after it! We can sneak up on his camp-fire and plug him while he's lounging on his backside. I'm pulling out with or without you, Reg!'

Reg Moss frowned, 'All right, all right,' he said disgustedly. 'I'll go along but let's get a bottle to take with us.'

When they stepped out of the saloon they were met by a man wearing a badge. 'You two hold on there for a minute.' Marshal Mike Meagher had his right hand on the grip of his holstered six-gun. 'I'll take that gun.' He motioned with his free hand to Reg Moss. Reg was powerless as he held a bottle of whiskey in his gun hand. Meagher stepped forward and lifted the gun from its holster.

Meagher looked both men over then said, 'Give me your names.'

'Charlie Roades,' . . . 'Reg Moss,' each man said in tandem.

'Where did you two come from?'

'We've been up to Abilene,' Reg said.

'Well, from the looks of the rigging on those horses I'd say you ain't been doing much in the way of herding cattle; no ropes, rain slickers and such. Where do you hail from?' Meagher asked.

'Out towards Baxter Springs,' Reg muttered.

'Ah, you're part of Ben Seldon's outfit,' Meagher said matter-of-factly.

'I reckon,' Reg acknowledged. Meagher's watchful eye caught a frowned grimace that Charlie Roades made.

'The man you're looking for is already gone,' Meagher offered, 'on his way back to Texas, I expect.' He looked to Charlie Roades, 'I don't know of any misdeeds you may have done nor do I have a quarrel with you. You can go about your business but your friend here is going to stay with us for a while. He owes the city of Wichita a debt.'

'What kind of debt, Marshal?' Roades managed.

'He owes a twenty-five dollar fine for raising hell in The Big Bull saloon late one night, not so long ago. And he'll also need to settle up some property damage he caused while busting up some furniture. He rode out of town, shooting up the storefronts as he went before anyone could stop him.' Meagher grinned. 'It seems that a dog always does return to his vomit!'

'He ain't got much money, Marshal,' Roades said. 'How long you figure before you let him go?'

'It works out to a dollar a day until the debt is paid,' Meagher said. 'You might as well go about your business unless you can come up with some cash to help him out.'

Roades nodded. 'I'll be on my way, Marshal.'

'You might as well take his bottle; he won't be using it,' Meagher said then watched as Reg Moss handed the bottle to Charlie. 'Oh, and before you go, take his horse over to the livery, I expect the horse won't be used for a while.'

CHAPTER 14

Sam had an edgy wariness about him as his horse settled down to a walk and plodded along. A while ago there was a feeling of people near and around him on all sides, now there was the feeling of solitude. He took good care that no one was following: looking to the right, to the left, then behind him. The edgy wariness began to fade as he left civilization behind and he became more relaxed in his watchfulness as he looked around. It was near sunset when he began looking for a place to camp for the night. Sam had chosen his route with the intention of not going toward Caldwell, the grubby little town sitting just north of the border before Indian Territory. If someone were trailing him that would be one of the first places a man hunter would expect him to go. Instead, he had been traveling in a south-easterly direction following the Arkansas River that flowed into and through Indian Territory on its course to the Mississippi. By following the river south he would eventually come to the old Shawnee trail and could follow that right through the territory and on into Dallas.

There was a line of tall cottonwoods lining the river so

he headed there to make his camp. He pulled the roan to a halt, then stepped down and loosened the cinch and pulled the saddle from the horse. He grappled in a saddle-bag and came out with a hobble which he placed on the horse's forelegs. Within a short time he had a small fire going, and by dark he had had a meal of fried potatoes and bacon along with some strong black coffee. Afterwards he cleaned the skillet using leaves and sand as a scrubber and river water to rinse clean. He banked the fire for the night then unrolled his bedding, took off his boots and gunbelt and lay down, pillowing his head on his saddle. He pulled his blanket up to his chin and put his hat over his face.

Sam lay there for half an hour in the darkness his eyes closed, but a nagging unease gnawed at him, preventing sleep. When the roan stamped a foot, Sam's eyes flew open. He reached out and grasped the handle of his gun, pulling it close to his stomach under the blanket. He slowly rotated his head looking for any intrusion. He could smell the river in its nocturnal silence on his left side, a wide open prairie to his right with a light wind blowing. Along the river-bank were numerous cottonwoods. If someone were looking to make an attack it would most likely come from near the trees which could be used as a screen or protection.

The fire had died down to a glow and it was dark enough that he figured he could slide out of his blanket without drawing any attention in the moonless night. Leaving his hat behind, he rolled into the darkness, six-gun ready.

Fifteen feet away, Sam lay flat on his belly as he stared

at his blanket and hat near the fire. He had stretched his gun arm out toward the bedroll and waited, straining to listen.

The roar of the rifle shot startled him. In the flash of the gun when fired, he had a brief outline of a man standing downriver, twenty paces away. Sam fired two shots at the muzzle flash then rolled quickly away from any reprisal. He had heard a grunt when he had fired then the thud of the man's body hitting the ground. Sam waited in the darkness, listening. He heard what sounded like moaning. After what seemed like an eternity but was really only less than five minutes, Sam stood with his gun at the ready. He walked forward cautiously in his stockinged feet toward the moaning. When he had taken about twenty steps, he stopped and struck a match. A man lay on his back with his arms wrapped around his stomach, his eyes closed, moaning lightly. The front of his shirt was bloody. Sam took the gun from the man's holster just as the match went out. He walked back to the camp-fire and donned his boots, strapped on his own gun then built up the fire. Returning to the downed man he took him under the arms and dragged him toward the fire. The man's eyes were still closed, seemingly unconscious from the move to the fire. Sam took his canteen, kneeled down and dribbled some water on the man's face, then let him drink a little. His eyes fluttered open and looked at Sam, then he closed his eyes again. He swallowed dryly, and was panting shallowly. 'I guess you got me good!'

Sam nodded. 'That I did, but you were trying to get me.'

The man's eyes opened again. 'I don't guess there's

much hope for me, is there?'

'I could take a look.'

'OK.'

Sam undid the man's shirt and did a quick examination and determined that both shots had taken the man in his stomach area and both had exited through his lower back. From the slimy gore extending from the gaping exit wounds on the man's back it was evident to Sam that he wouldn't last long.

'No, I don't guess there's much hope.'

The man's eyes closed again. 'I didn't think so because my guts are on fire.'

Sam wetted a cloth and dabbed at the man's face and slapped his jaws lightly to see if he would wake. The eyes fluttered.

'Who are you?' Sam asked.

'Charlie Roades,' he said, in a halting voice.

'Well, you were trying to shoot me; why?'

Roades did not answer, but asked instead, 'How long you figure I got?'

'It'll be a short time, Charlie. I can't help you, but I can sit with you for a while, if you want.'

'You'd do that for me after I tried to shoot you? Most would have shot me again and ridden off. I'm sorry I tried to shoot you, but . . but the reward. Ben said he'd pay it to anyone who got you.'

'A thousand dollars, is what I heard,' Sam said.

Charlie nodded. 'More money than I ever saw before.' Then he grimaced, as pain racked his body drawing him into a fetal position.

'Is there anybody else out looking for me?' Sam asked.

Charlie drew in a ragged breath. 'I'm alone, but I expect half the boys in Kansas are looking. My partner's in jail in Wichita. We just missed you there but' – he gasped a raspy breath then continued – 'we spread the word in Newton. Wink Robbins went up to Abilene. The old man is mad as hell and wants you real bad.'

'You would have had to take my body someplace in order to collect on that reward money. Where might that be?' Sam asked.

Charlie's eyes rolled. 'Back to Ben's place near Baxter Springs. I'm s'posed to meet him there Saturday night.'

'Baxter Springs; I've heard that before. North, south?

'Five or six miles north; near to the cattle trail. You got any whiskey, Sam?'

'I don't. Wish I did; might ease the pain some, but I got a smoke if you want.' When Charlie nodded, Sam busied rolling a cigarette then took a smoldering stick from the fire and lit it. He drew a puff then put the end in Charlie's lips. Charlie drew a little then moved his head indicating that was enough.

'There's a bottle in my saddle-bag,' Charlie said. 'My horse ain't too far away. I'd sure like a taste before I go. He's a good horse; I never called him anything but hoss.'

'I'll get it, Charlie,' Sam said.

Sam took a lighted limb as a torch and found the horse a distance away. The animal, a sorrel, tried to shy away when Sam approached, but nickered and settled when Sam gave a reassuring pat to his muzzle. He swung into the saddle and walked the horse to the camp, then tied the horse and rummaged in the saddle-bags until he found the full bottle of whiskey. He uncorked it and took a swig himself, then went over to where Charlie was lying. The eyes were open but frozen in death. Sam knelt and slapped at the man's lower jaw to no avail. Charlie Roades had died. 'Damn!' Sam muttered, then sat down by the fire and took another pull on the bottle. He sat for a long time alternately looking at the fire then at the body of Charles Roades while continuing to sip. The more he thought and drank the madder he got. J.D. Seldon, by his own making, had died in Ellsworth for no good reason. Thanks to Ben Seldon two more men had died: Jay Bradford in Wichita, and now Charlie Roades here on this windswept plain by the river. Sleep was out of the question. He was of a mind to pack up and leave this place right now, but it was so dark he knew it would be hard on his horse to travel in the pitch blackness.

He needed to dispose of the body. Burying the man where he lay was as good a place as any he figured. But he had no digging tools and there weren't exactly any rocks around on the prairie to collect and cover over him either. He could just ride off and let the coyotes and buzzards have a go at the body but he didn't like that idea. If nothing else he could roll the body into the river, which wasn't exactly roaring fast.

Sam got to his feet then went to Roades's saddle and took off the bedroll. He wrapped Roades in it so that only his booted feet were sticking out. Finding no rope in Roades's gear, he reached down to his own saddle and plucked a rope from it, tying it around the body and throwing the loose rope over a cottonwood limb about twelve feet off the ground and tied it off to the horse's saddle horn and led it a few feet until the body was about six feet off the ground. He untied the rope from the saddle horn then attached it to the trunk of the tree. The bundle swung back and forth as Sam unsaddled the sorrel and hobbled it so it wouldn't wander off in the night. Satisfied, he returned to the little fire and made it up. At least he had the body up and away from night-roaming scavengers that were sure to prowl around, and it was out of his sight, for now anyway. He took another pull on the whiskey bottle and rolled himself a smoke. When the smoke was down to a stub, he threw it into the fire then laid his head on his saddle. If the stars had been out he could have looked at them, but all that was above him was darkness. He tried to clear his mind of the shooting and think of Ellen Riggs; how lovely she was and the kiss she had given him. The memory of that kiss lingered and gave him a warm feeling. Would she really travel all the way to Fort Worth or Dallas? She hadn't said she would, but indicated that she might. He scarcely knew her, yet he wanted badly to see her again. Sam's eyes closed while he fabricated images of Ellen in his mind and inadvertently fell asleep

CHAPTER 15

Wink Robbins had gotten into Abilene just before dusk on Tuesday. He stayed that night in a shoddy hotel and spent most of the next day asking about Sam Hall. He'd asked everyone he could think of which included hotel clerks, livery operators, mercantile clerks, waitresses at the cafés, and bartenders at the saloons, but no one knew of Hall or his whereabouts. He told of the reward only to those whom he judged might have an interest, figuring it would be a wasted effort on some clerks, waitresses and whores. He told bartenders and anyone in particular who had the look of wary eyed men who might be on the dodge. No one seemed to have any information. Wink lounged in a saloon until late, gabbing with some local cowboys about how things had changed since the herds weren't being sold and shipped from Abilene any longer.

At daylight, Wink had breakfast and left the restaurant after three cups of strong coffee. Satisfied that Hall had not been there and that he had spread the word about the reward as much as possible, he figured it time to leave town. He did so, heading his horse due south towards

Newton to check if Reg and Charlie had done what Ben Seldon had sent them out to do.

It was mid-afternoon when he rode into dusty Newton. The town wasn't any busier than Abilene had been, but then there weren't any herds coming to either town. No herds also meant there weren't any free-spending, hell-raising cowboys to put things in an uproar. Ellsworth and Wichita had taken all of that business. The clerk at the hotel where Wink booked a room said that he remembered Reg Moss by the description with which Wink furnished him.

'Yeah they stayed here two nights. They just left this morning. That Reg fella sure did like to yammer. He kept saying how he was going to get a hold of some big money pretty soon. His partner was OK, kinda quiet, I guess.'

Wink got the same story at two different saloons. 'One of them was gambling and drinking freely while the other one was more reserved, talking to others but not rambling on like his partner did,' one bartender recalled.

At the other saloon the bartender shook his head. 'I remember the mouth, telling of a reward that he intended to collect. He didn't say how he was going to go about getting it. You might ask some of the crowd later on though, he could have said something to someone.'

The next day around noon Wink arrived in Wichita. He rode straight to the livery intending to check his horse in and see to its care before roaming about. There was a horse in the corral that caught his eye. There wasn't anything special about it, being an ordinary sorrel, except for the fact that he was certain that the horse belonged to Reg Moss. He dismounted and walked close to the corral fence to get a better look and sure enough when the horse turned he displayed a big 'H' that had been branded on its side. Most horses were branded on a hip or way back on the side away from where a cinch might rub but not this horse; he had been branded right in the middle, suggesting perhaps the identifying mark had been done by someone who didn't know the first thing about branding an animal. That was Reg Moss's horse for sure.

Wink looked over the other horses in the corral but couldn't spot the one Charlie Roades called his own. When the liveryman came out to see of his want, Wink asked, 'Feed and a stall for the night?'

'Four bits,' the man said.

'One night will be fine,' Wink said, then asked, 'That sorrel over there, with the H brand, you know of the owner?'

The man glanced at the horse. 'Fella who brought that horse in said that the man's name is Reg Moss, I wrote it down in my ledger. He said Moss was in jail and that he might be there for a while. He didn't say anything more and rode off.'

'If Reg gets out of jail and can't pay the feed bill, what happens then?' Wink asked.

'It's four bits a day whether he can pay or not. When the bill gets to thirty dollars then the horse automatically belongs to me. Judge O'connor said I could shorten it to thirty days if I wanted, but it works out OK the way it is. Most of the actual owners pay up after a few days and settle the bill with their men later. Is that fella a friend of yours?'

'I wouldn't call him a friend, but I know who he is and the outfit that he works for. Have you heard why he's in jail?' Wink asked.

'The word is that he busted up one of the saloons a few weeks ago and the marshal happened to recognize him and took him in. I expect he'll have to pay a fine to get out of jail.'

Wink smiled. 'Might be the best thing for him, a little jail time. Maybe he'll sober up. That fella who brought the horse in, was he kind of a thin-looking guy with wrinkled clothes?'

'Yeah, that's him.'

'You say he rode off. Did he say where he was going?'

'He didn't say; seemed like he was in a hurry though, not much on palavering.'

'Hey, thanks for the info. I'll see you in the morning to pick up my horse.' Wink reached into his pocket and handed the man fifty cents. 'I like to pay ahead,' he said, then handed the man the reins and walked off. He thought about Charlie Roades as he walked along, wondering if Charlie had gone back to Ben's place. Maybe he had found Sam Hall and went to get Ben's help but that didn't add up. Charlie was the type of guy who had enough sand that he would have attempted to take Hall on his own. Hell, a thousand dollar payoff was an awfully good-looking hole card and a powerful incentive. Just knowing about the reward would cause a man to do things and take chances that he normally wouldn't do. Charlie for sure didn't need any interference from Reg Moss and had left the man in jail. Wink thought about that too, he wasn't about to bail Moss out, maybe Ben would consider it but most likely he wouldn't.

Wink booked a room then walked into the first saloon

that he came to and ordered a rye. He stood before the bar letting the drink burn its way down when he heard the name of Sam Hall spoken by someone in a group further down the bar. Wink ordered another drink then picked it up and walked down to stand next to the group. 'I just got into town. What can you tell me about this Sam Hall?' he asked.

Two men tried to talk over each other attempting to be the first to get the word out about the shootout that had taken place. Suddenly the bar was abuzz with talk about Sam Hall.

'He was here and we didn't even know it, until after the shootout,' one man said. Another said, 'Be damned if he wasn't fast; he outdrew that kid like it was nothing.'

'Shoot a man down, did he?' Wink pried.

'Some young fella nobody ever heard of had it figured that he was a gun-slick and called Hall out right there in front of the hotel. Hall told him to go away, but the kid drew his gun instead. His shot missed, but Hall got him with one shot right in the middle of the chest. Before the shooting started the kid had said he was trying to collect some kind of a bounty on Hall, but others say the reward wasn't put up by the law,' said a tall man, wearing clothes that looked as if he were a drummer of some sort.

'It was most likely a relative of that other fella J.D. Seldon that Hall shot down just a few days ago is what I heard,' a different voice said.

'Where's Hall at now?' Wink asked.

A short, fat man chomping on a cigar took the smoke out of his mouth then spoke up. 'The marshal ran him out of town soon after the shooting. Word is he took off for Texas where he came from, Dallas or Fort Worth, I heard.'

CHAPTER 16

Sam woke up with a foul taste in his mouth. He sat up and looked around for his canteen. Locating it, he took a mouthful and spat it out then lifted the canteen for some to swallow. He was a little sleep sandy-eyed so he poured some of the water into his hand then splashed and rubbed the water over his face. The cool morning breeze along with the water was bracing enough to awaken him fully. Sam stood and looked around the campsite. His eyes immediately went to the hanging blanket-covered body, and the reality of last night flooded his memory. He was glad that he had covered Charlie Roades for he did not want to look at that sorrowful face again.

The sky was a leaden gray with heavy clouds and the wind began to pick up blowing leaves and debris swirling around. He could smell rain, far off perhaps, but it looked as if it would begin soon. The horses were standing quietly; both stared at him expectantly. Sam had a little grain in a sack so he scooped some out and piled a handful on the ground before each animal. Both horses began licking and munching contentedly.

If he worked quickly, Sam figured, he could get break-fast for himself before the rain came. He stirred at the fire but it was dead, so he searched around and found enough dry twigs and leaves to kindle a new one, then broke some small limbs over his knee. With the help of the increasing wind fanning the flames he soon had a decent fire going. He put on a small coffee pot and a skillet for frying bacon and bread then he busied rolling up his bedding and sad-dling his horse while waiting. When the food was ready, Sam ate his fill and sat sipping the last of the strong brewed coffee just as a few sprinkles began to fall. The raindrops seemed exceedingly loud as they pelted his hat and shoulders.

He rolled around in his mind as to what to do with the body of Charlie Roades. He needed to act quickly before the coming rain made things miserable. With purpose in mind, he stood and swirled the dregs of his coffee out of the cup. He cleaned up the cooking and eating gear and stowed them away then began saddling Roades's horse. It was docile enough under his pushing and guiding hands and was soon in position under the bundled body. Sam lowered the body on to the saddle with only a mild protest from the horse, and tied the stiffened hands and booted feet together under the horse's belly with a hobble rope. He tugged on the bundle to see how it would ride. Satisfied that it was firm enough, he put Roades's holster and six-gun in one of the saddle-bags and returned the saddle gun to the boot. Now the dead man had everything that he had ridden in with right on his own horse's back. Sam took the reins to Charlie's horse and knotted the ends into a D ring on the back of his own saddle. That way the horse would follow without Sam having to constantly give him a pull to go. He had just finished when the rain began to come faster and was suddenly a steady downpour. Sam donned his rain slicker and hurriedly mounted before his saddle became too wet.

When on the cattle trail, rain was always a nuisance but not a deterrent; the cattle were kept moving rain or shine. Sam had spent many days such as this hunkered miserably on his horse while the rain continued all day long. This looked exactly like one of those days. The only saving grace to the rain was that it would obliterate his tracks, making it next to impossible for others attempting to follow him. It would also give him cover. He could make good time without the worry of being seen from a distance. Sam looked back at the horse behind him wishing he had a canvas to cover the body; having gone through the man's belongings he found that Charlie didn't even have a rain slicker in his meager possessions.

Sam turned his horse to walk along near the river-bank with the other horse following. His mind was made up. He wasn't about to spend from now to eternity looking over his shoulder to see if someone was coming after him. Charlie Roades had trailed him, apparently alone, but he was now certain that others would also follow. An attempt to track him was almost guaranteed, the only question being when; possibly as soon as tonight, tomorrow or later, but they would follow; hard, ruthless men, blinded by the promise of a thousand dollar bounty. If Sam was spotted, he would most likely be shot on sight. He wasn't going to wait and see if that would happen.

Sam did not like being chased one bit, as if he were a

wanted criminal on the dodge from the law. And running, well, that was something that he had ever done before and definitely was not what he had intended to do from the beginning of this débâcle. Sam had been ordered to leave two different towns, but he wasn't about to run and hide like a child after doing something wrong. Sam had only done what he thought was right in order to stay alive and there was nothing wrong in that. Sam wondered if Ben Seldon would have offered the bounty on him even if he had not taken the reward on J.D. and decided that he most likely would have. Now whether it was out of loyalty to his brother, or just plain meanness on Ben Seldon's part didn't matter. The fact was that the offer had been made and now there were men whom he did know out to shoot him down as if he were a rabid dog.

He decided he wasn't going to run away and hide; by damn, he would deliver Roades's body right back to Ben Seldon's place where the man had come from! Oh, he would not go riding in to Seldon's front yard in broad day-light; that would be suicide. If, however, he were to allow the horse to deliver the body under the cover of darkness, then the message would be clear: Sam Hall is not so easy to kill and will fight back when necessary! The more he thought about it, the more it felt like it was the right thing to do. Sam had always figured that when in a fight and your opponent throws a punch at you, then the most logical thing to do was to punch back, but harder. Sometimes that action alone was enough to end a quarrel.

He didn't expect Ben Seldon to call off the chase by the arrival of Roades's body tied to a horse. Sam had not started this fight but he would see it to conclusion or die trying. If any others saw fit to come after him, then he wasn't going to give them an easy time of collecting that bounty. Sam had figured that if Charlie's horse was led near to Seldon's place and turned loose, the animal would most likely head straight to the familiar corral.

For now he needed to cross the river and head east to locate the Shawnee Trail without being seen. Once he located the trail, he could simply follow it north to Baxter Springs instead of south to Dallas like he had originally figured to do when he left Wichita.

It took about an hour before Sam found a likely place to cross the river. The horses walked almost halfway across the murky water before they had to swim and it was only a few yards before their feet found the bottom again. By reckoning, Sam turned his horse to what he considered to be due east, as the sun obscured by the clouds could not be used as a direction finder.

Hours passed as Sam rode along. He thought about Leroy Hagen out there roaming free somewhere, while Danny Helms lay in his grave. About Ben Seldon who had offered a stinking bounty which had already caused the death of Jay Bradford in Wichita and now Charlie Roades here on the plains – their blood was on Ben Seldon's hands. The thoughts brought him to fury and greatly increased his thirst for vengeance causing him to prod the horses along faster.

Sam figured that sooner or later he would have to face Ben Seldon, but he did not want to face an army of Seldon's men at the same time. Right now he didn't know how many men that amounted to. He figured that the only way to handle a pack of wolves was to take them out one at a time, not the whole pack at once. Sam would have to work that out later.

Sam looked off to the flat plains around him. The country was ideal to herd cattle through; flatter than flat and covered with grass feed with few trees to get in the way of movement. Now that he was trying to remain unseen, he found the countryside offensive. Out on the plains, on a clear day, one could see anything that moved at a great distance, the only cover being the scrawny trees that grew along the river and bushes near the puny creeks. Thankfully, the rain had changed that, bringing visibility down to a few hundred yards at best.

He rode all day in the steady drizzle stopping occasionally to get off and walk the kinks out of his legs. He figured that the distance from the river to the Shawnee trail was most likely over a hundred miles. It would take all of today and half of tomorrow before he could locate the trail, then another half day before he would get up to Baxter Springs.

Just before total darkness forced him to stop, he made his camp next to a creek lined with bushes as there were no trees to be found. The rain had slacked some, but that didn't make his cold camp any cheerier. He wanted coffee, but there was nothing with which to build a fire, so he contented himself with some dried apricots, slivers of jerky and some hard tack washed down with water. The horses were wet and miserable but he couldn't do anything about that, other than stripping off the saddles and letting them graze. Everything was wet, so he unrolled his bedding and spread his blanket over a bush and burrowed underneath to at least get the rain out of his face. Remembering the whiskey, he got it out of the saddle-bag and swallowed three long drinks of the fiery stuff. At least it warmed his insides. Then he curled up and attempted a listless sleep. Sam startled awake each time one of the horses moved or stamped a foot. It was the beginning of dawn when he sat up. Though not rested, he figured that he might as well get up and get the horses saddled and ready for another day. It was still drizzling. He wrung out the blanket he had used as a tent, rolled it up and stowed it away. Taking the little sack of grain that held no more than a couple of handfuls, he gave half to each horse.

'Someday soon you'll get a lot more grain, some hay and a dry place to sleep,' he said soothingly to the horses. He wondered if horses, supposedly being dumb brutes, could actually understand man's language or only reacted to being directed by a prod, or bribed with food.

After both horses were saddled, he then had a heck of a time getting the stiffened body back on to the horse. Charlie weighed about 150 pounds, and Sam, though strong, was almost at the point of exhaustion from repeated attempts to lift the body on to the horse. Eventually, he was able to drape and tie the body over the saddle tying the hands and feet together under the horse's belly and was ready to ride by full daylight.

It was mid-afternoon when he found wide trails hoofed out and littered with the remnants of dried or washed-out cow patties. It had to be the Shawnee Trail. He turned the animals in a northern direction and continued on. Once he thought he spotted a movement up ahead. He brought the animals to a halt and waited, shielding his eyes in an attempt to see what it was. He spotted a coyote slogging along unconcerned and before long the scavenger trotted out of Sam's sight.

The horses were wet and in need of a rest and time to graze. Sam dismounted and walked for a while, then remounted, determined to stop when and if he came upon some trees that would give him cover. It was late afternoon when he came upon a fence. In the distance he could see some buildings, a spiral of smoke drifting up from a cabin's chimney, and a corral and barn. As badly as Sam would like to have ridden in and sought shelter for the night, he knew he had to keep going. He turned the horses aside and rode on. If he could see the buildings then it was possible for the inhabitants to see him.

Soon he came to a road that seemed to come from the farm he had just passed. He followed it north for a ways until he came to a crossroads. A signpost with an arrow pointing west read *Baxter Springs 2 miles.* Underneath was another signpost pointing east reading *Joplin 11 miles.*

Sam's heart gave a little flutter. He was close to his destination now and that meant that he had to be extra vigilant lest he be observed. He gigged a spur to his horse's flank and encouraged the animals to a lope. He needed to find an out of sight place to hole up until darkness came and he could continue. He didn't know how he would be able to locate Ben Seldon's place, but Charlie had said it was about five or six miles north of Baxter Springs near to the Shawnee Trail.

Sam kept the horses headed in a northerly direction and rode the better part of an hour before he spotted some trees and bushes up ahead. On closer inspection, there was a creek running through a fairly deep ravine which would be as good a spot to rest the horses as he could ask for. The ravine was deep enough that the horses' bodies were not silhouetted. Only their heads, when raised, would show above the sides. It was at least an hour before dark by the time he brought the animals to stop. He dismounted and hobbled the animals so they would not wander away then removed the bridles so they could graze at their leisure on the long grass growing along the creek bed. Sam was exhausted, but was unable to rest just yet. The horses needed only to rest for an hour or so, then, when it was dark, he would try to locate Seldon's place. He took out the whiskey bottle. Maybe the burn it created going down would relax him a little.

CHAPTER 17

Wink Robbins was up early and had a twenty-five cent breakfast of biscuits, gravy and coffee. Afterward he left the restaurant and headed to the livery having already checked out of the hotel. It was raining lightly and that would make for a miserable day of riding. He had told Ben that he would see him on Saturday and he would make the ride, rain or not.

Wink spent his travelling time from Wichita to Baxter Springs in the same misery that Sam Hall had. The incessantly drizzling rain made sloppy traveling and making a camp was less than convenient or desirable. He had himself spent time herding cattle in such conditions and wouldn't repeat that again, if he had a choice. It was one of the reasons he had hooked up with Ben Seldon in order to get out of the grind that most cowboys fell into. Normally the pay a cowboy could expect at the end of a trail drive was subject to the boss's mood as to whether he received a bonus or just the regular thirty dollars a month. The number of animals lost on a drive was a factor as was the length of time it had taken to make the trip and, of course, the price the animals were sold for. With Ben Seldon things were different: it was commonplace for riders to earn fifty to a hundred dollars a month without spending eighteen hours a day in the saddle. Sure, Ben dealt in stolen cattle, but he didn't ask anything of his men that he wouldn't do himself. Often Ben would pay out generous shares to everyone after a delivery was made, provided those taking the chances kept their mouths shut and did as he had ordered.

Wink arrived at the Seldon farmhouse at about the same time that Sam Hall had stopped in the ravine, not far away, where he was waiting for darkness. He rode his horse straight to the barn and, once inside, stripped the saddle and bridle then moved the horse to a stall and gave him some hay.

When he opened the front door he saw Ben sitting in his customary chair near the pot-bellied stove.

Ben nodded. 'You're the first one back, Wink. I knew you'd keep your word. Did you see hide or hair of those other two?'

'Reg Moss is in jail in Wichita. I reckon that marshal he spoke of caught up with him.'

'Is that what happened?' Ben asked.

'I didn't talk to him. The word is he owes a fine and it's costing four bits a day to keep his horse at the livery. Hall had been there though. I guess some young fella got word of the bounty in Newton and he caught up to Hall in Wichita before Reg and Charlie showed up there. He called out Hall in the street. They say Sam Hall obliged the fellow; out-drew him and left him dead in the street. That Marshal Meagher witnessed the whole thing; said it was self-defense, but ordered Hall to leave town anyway. He'd already left before I got there.'

Ben sat back in his chair. 'So Hall was in Wichita all along Reg, and Charlie let some snot nose try and take him? Well, if Reg's in jail, I don't give a damn. The bastard can rot there, far as I'm concerned. He's been a hindrance for some time now. What about Charlie, did you see him?'

'No, I didn't see him. The fella at the livery said Charlie had brought in Reg's horse to board him, then said that Charlie took off in a hurry. I figured he came back here to let you know and get some help, but I guess it looks most likely he went after Sam Hall on his own.'

'Well, he ain't showed up here,' Ben said. 'Musta gone after Hall. That Charlie's got the guts to try something like that, but if you're saying that Sam Hall outdrew and killed a man in broad daylight, then I figure Charlie might be biting off a little more than he can chew. Charlie thinks he's fast with a six-gun, but I've seen others who could best him. Who knows though, he might get lucky. Any word as to where Hall went?'

'A couple fellas I talked to, said someone overheard Hall tell one of the deputies that he was heading back to Texas, where he came from. Fort Worth and Dallas were mentioned.'

Ben grunted. 'Texas is a big place and pretty damned far away, but it's straight south of here to Dallas. We'd most likely get more takers in one town down in Texas, than in the whole state of Kansas. It wouldn't be the worst thing to go down there, and nose around a bit. If nothing else we can find out how many herds are headed this way. We might be able to run off a few head for our own purposes so's it wouldn't be a wasted trip. I'll think on that some more. Now that you were able to spread word of the reward, do you figure you got any takers? Is there anybody going out to try and track Hall down?'

Wink poured himself a cup of coffee and took a chair across from Ben. He took a sip, winced from the heat of it, then set the cup down. 'I didn't find anyone frothing at the bit to get on the trail. It might have been a different story if we'd known where Hall took off to, but most of the ones I spoke to only had a mild interest. I think they were more interested in doing a little thieving, with a lesser risk, than the possibility of facing a gun-slick. It takes a different kind of individual to go man-hunting; one who's cocksure of his own abilities; hungry for a name for himself as well as quick money. It takes the kind of man who isn't afraid of another's reputation; the sort of individual as that fella Hall shot down in Wichita. How about you, Ben, were you able to get anyone interested?'

Ben smiled broadly. 'Maybe so, and right close by too. I ran into Nick Shores and Rob Bonhart over in Joplin. You remember Nick, don't you? He rode with us here when all the big herds were going up the Shawnee Trail to Sedalia. The pickings were pretty easy in those days. A man could scare up a hundred head from a bedded down herd by just waiting until dark and getting them herded to our north pasture. When most all the big herds were diverted over to Abilene and other places, then Nick wasn't content with the few dollars that I could offer and went out on his own. Rob Bonhart is good with his gun. I saw him outdraw a card cheat up in Sedalia a few years ago. He shot the man down then walked over to the cheat's side of the table and drank the rest of the dead man's whiskey. He's that cold; fast and accurate, too. Anyway those two were just finishing up a freight hauling job and said they'd be over in the morning to see if anyone's brought word on Hall's location.'

CHAPTER 18

Sam had taken a long swig of the whiskey, gasping as the liquid travelled down his throat. He was seated on the ground, holding the bottle in his right hand. His eye caught a sudden movement behind him and on his right side. He was startled and was just on the verge of dropping the bottle and grabbing for his gun when someone stepped over the edge and began to walk down the bank of the ravine. The figure appeared to be unarmed. Sam set the bottle down and put his hand on the butt of his gun, figuring that if this was someone who was after him, it would have already been too late. The person was dressed in work denims covered by a knee-length rain slicker and wore a slouch hat, which obscured his face. Though full bodied, it appeared to be a woman because of the long gray hair streaked with a darker colour, hanging down past the shoulders. Sam stood as she walked toward him, her laced brogans crunching on creek bed gravel. The woman's face was ruddy red and wind burnt and showed the beginnings of crows' feet at the corners of her eyes. She was older, fiftyish maybe, thick in body and bosom and appeared at home in the work clothes which Sam figured were most likely her husband's.

She walked up to within ten feet of where Sam stood. 'Are you planning on trying to camp in this ravine?' she asked.

Sam did his best to give a smile. 'I was just hoping to let my animals have a rest before I move on. They had a long day. I didn't see any buildings about and wasn't sure where I was at. I didn't mean to trespass. I won't be long,' he said, hoping she wouldn't make a fuss over the body bundled on the saddle but there was hardly a way that she would not notice it.

'The house and barn are up there.' She pointed north where the creek was flowing from. 'You didn't see it because of all this brush, but if you had ridden out a few yards you would have been able to see them. I don't get any visitors that don't use the road and I keep a keen eye out for predators looking to get at what few chickens and critters I have. I noticed you coming a ways off and watched when you went into the ravine. When you didn't come out I figured you were set on making camp. It wouldn't be a neighborly thing to leave a traveler out in the rain.'

The woman looked past him to the horses and the body. 'Looks like you're loaded down. Are you a lawman?'

'No ma'am, I'm not. I'm just going to deliver the body back to its kin.'

She glanced at it again then looked straight into Sam's eyes. 'If you don't mind my asking, who might they be?'

Sam fidgeted, for he didn't want to have to explain everything, but it seemed he had no choice. 'I was told that he came from Ben Seldon's place. I'm just not quite sure where that is exactly.'

The woman gave him disdainful look. 'Is Ben Seldon a friend of yours?'

Sam shook his head from side to side. 'I sure wouldn't say that, because I never met him and the man lying across that saddle was no friend either. Fact is, I'm the one who did that fella in. He was trying to shoot me so I shot him before he could finish his task! Ben Seldon is the one who sent him after me.'

'And who are you?' she asked.

Sam thought about giving himself a different name but when he opened his mouth it came out as natural as it should. 'The name is Sam Hall, ma'am. I'm just a cattle drover from Texas, but Ben Seldon got it into his head that I'm a bounty hunter who killed his brother, and I won't deny that I had a part in it. I just didn't purposely go after J.D. for the reward.'

The woman got a look of astonishment on her face. 'I read that in the newspaper about J.D. You're the man who got him, eh?' Sam nodded.

'And now Ben's sent that bunch out to get revenge on you?'

Sam nodded again. 'He's offered a thousand dollars reward to anyone who brings me to him dead or alive.'

'My name is Miriam Holder and I'm right pleased to meet you, Sam Hall. I want you to know that I have no qualms about you using my place to stay out of Ben Seldon's sight. I sure wouldn't be delivering that body in broad daylight though, if I were you.'

'I hadn't planned on it. It will be dark soon and I'll get

the job done then,' Sam noted.

She walked over to stand next to the body. 'Do you mind if I have a look?' Sam shook his head. She knelt down and uncovered the face. She looked at it, wincing when she did, then covered it carefully again and stood. 'That's Charlie Roades. I thought that horse looked familiar.

Sam was somewhat amazed, 'You knew this man?'

'I knew *of* him; we ain't exactly on tea-drinking terms, but I know some of the old bunch that's been running with Ben for years. Sometimes, during trail driving season, there are others who come and go to Ben's at all hours. You're real close to your destination. Ben's place is right next to mine.' She pointed off to the west. 'About two miles over there. If it wasn't raining you could see the house and outbuildings in the distance. After you rested, were you just going to lead that horse over there?'

Sam shook his head. 'Not exactly. I had it figured that his horse was familiar enough with the layout and would go in on his own if I led him in close.'

Miriam nodded. 'You're most likely right. I expect that he'd go on over there right now, if you were to let him loose. Need to do that right soon: the body is starting to bloat in this warm rain and it's going to start stinking right quick.'

'Yes'm, I'll do that soon as it gets dark.'

Miriam looked at him and asked, 'What are you going to do afterwards? Where are you going, and what are you expecting Ben Seldon to do about it?'

'I figured to go into Baxter Springs and see about getting a room there. I was hoping to rest up for a day or so and see if I had Seldon's attention. Most likely a saloon 'keep in town would know all the particulars inside of a day or so. And if Ben gets word that I'm in town and decides on coming after me, it might just as well be there as any other place. I tried to go on my way and mind my own business, but the next thing I knew there were people looking to kill me. I'm not running so that's why I'm here; to settle this thing, one way or the other.'

The woman looked at the ground then back up. 'I wouldn't be of a mind to get in a hurry, if I was you. Baxter Springs would be the first place they are going to look. That's exactly what Ben would think you'd do and I don't believe that he is apt to wait until you've rested up. Once they get possession of the body, Ben, and whatever men he has around, will most likely be crawling all over town tonight. Ben's been in this country long enough that he knows everybody and they know him, which means they would side with Ben out of fear of the man and what he might do if they didn't.'

Sam nodded his head. 'I suppose that you're right, Mrs Holder, maybe I haven't thought this thing through like I should. You know more about your neighbor than I do, but it sure sounds like you don't hold much reverence for him.'

'It's Miriam and I'll tell you all about the Seldons later on, Sam, but for now let's get that body and these animals into my barn and out of sight. You can rest up some and, after a spell, when it's good and dark, you can finish your business. This camping in a creek-bed is bad on the rheumatism. I got some hot coffee back at the house. Come on, I'll help you lead the animals to the barn.'

Sam was, to say the least, a little bit flabbergasted. Not only had he found out where Ben Seldon's place was located but here was a stranger more than willing to help out and give him shelter.

Sam put the bridle on his horse while Miriam put the bridle on the other then began to lead the animal away, Sam following close behind, stopping only when Miriam had paused to open the barn doors.

Once inside the barn, Miriam led Roades's horse underneath a pulley hanging from a rope that led to the loft for lifting hay. 'Might as well give 'em rest even if it's only for an hour or so,' Miriam said, and the two of them pulled the body off the horse. They stripped the horses of saddles and bridles placing the tack over stall railings to dry. Miriam scooped a small amount of grain into a manger. The horses stepped right up and began licking the grain greedily. 'We can give your horse his fill when we get back, but we shouldn't give Charlie's very much so that he will go home when we turn him loose,' Miriam said.

Sam took up a gunny sack lying nearby and began wiping the animals down as they ate. Miriam began to move toward the open doors speaking to Sam over her shoulder as she closed them, 'Come up to the house when you're done; I'll get a fresh pot to brewing. You don't need to knock; just come on in, there's nobody around but Luther and me.'

Sam wondered who Luther was, perhaps her husband, and if he would give the same amount of kindly consideration to a stranger who showed up in a rainstorm packing a dead man with him. Still wary, he pulled his saddle gun from the boot and wiped off the water then headed to the house.

Inside was warm and pleasant with decent furniture situated about the room. Most dwellings that he had seen along the cattle trails were furnished with homemade pieces fabricated from poles and crates. These were obviously factory made and imported from some distant eastern place and had been well cared for, glowing with a recent sheen of polish. Sam stood just inside the door. He felt out of place and fearful that he would mess up something, that he would drip on to the braided rug when he was standing. Miriam emerged through a door from what he was presumed was the kitchen. 'Don't mind your wet things, Sam. Take your hat and coat and put them near the stove to dry. The coffee will be ready right soon.'

Miriam held out a towel to Sam to dry himself then disappeared back into the kitchen. Sam dried his face and hands and remained standing by the stove until Miriam extended a steaming coffee mug to him. He took it gratefully and, at her bidding, sat on a ladder-backed chair while she seated herself on a stuffed couch. 'Once you get some hot coffee in you and dry out some you'll feel a lot better,' she said.

'I thank you, Miriam. I just don't want to be a burden.'

'You're not, Sam. It's like I indicated earlier, I don't hold to the way Ben Seldon has done things for a long time now. I'll tell you all about it tonight after we get Charlie Roades on his way.'

It sounded to Sam as if Miriam had suddenly become his partner without being asked. 'I hope I'll be able to move in close enough to see that the horse gets to where he should be without me being seen,' Sam said then added, 'I reckon I'd prefer not to face the consequences in daylight.'

'We need to head up north past Morrison's then circle back down and come in on the west side. That provides the best cover. No need to worry about tracks as long as this rain continues, but coming in from that direction will further confuse them for sure. I know every creek-bed and ravine for miles around. Don't worry, Sam, I'll make sure you're not seen,' Miriam assured him. She held a blank expression on her face then said, 'I'd like to help, Sam.'

He figured there would be no arguing with this head-strong woman so he nodded. 'That would be fine, Miriam.'

'You sit here and have some more coffee while I get supper ready for Luther. It's already cooked, I made a stew earlier. I just need to dish it up and take it to him. You and I can eat later when we get back.'

Sam now figured that Luther was most likely a hired hand, but did not want to ask for fear of being too inquisitive. He was tired and could certainly stand a decent meal but he was edgy and wanting to finish the chore that he had assigned himself.

Miriam came into the room carrying a cloth-covered tray. She paused at the door. 'I know you're raring to go, but an hour or so is not going to matter. It'll be full dark in a little while and it will take a bit of riding to put us in position to release that horse. I'll be but a minute, Sam. Luther is most likely wondering where I'm at. He's used to eating at the same time every day.'

Sam nodded then went back to his chair by the stove.

CHAPTER 19

When Ben Seldon, Wink Robbins and Leroy Hagen heard the hoofbeats outside, they presumed they heralded Nick Shore and Rob Bonhart's expected arrival, so didn't bother to get up and look. Nick had lived there for a time, a while back, so Ben figured the men would head straight to the barn to see to their horses' needs before coming into the house. All sat waiting for the pair to pound up the steps and open the door. After more than adequate time had passed for the men to do their chores, Ben looked over to the door. 'I wonder what's keeping them?' he muttered.

Leroy was standing near the stove to Ben's left. 'You want me to go and see, Ben?'

'Yeah, that would be fine, Leroy,' Ben said. Leroy walked over and took a lantern from a peg on the wall, lit the lantern's wick then adjusted the flame. He set the lantern down while he put on his rain slicker, then, lantern in hand, he walked out the door and clomped across the porch and down the steps. It was dark enough that he could only see a short distance in front of where

127

he held the light. The rain was still drizzling as it had been for the past two days as he crossed the seventy-five yards to the barn and corral off to one side.

Leroy fell down in the mud twice in his haste to get back to the house. He had dropped the lantern after the second fall and left it lying where it fell. Slipping and sliding, he hurtled towards the lamplight glowing orange and yellow through windows on either side of the door.

Leroy was scared and shocked, but not speechless. He began yelling before he reached the steps, 'Ben! Ben! It's Charlie Roades! He's dead!'

There was the immediate thudding of boots on the floorboards, then the door was flung open. Ben Seldon's big frame came out the door on to the covered porch. 'What the hell are you yelling about?'

Leroy scurried up the steps to stand in front of him. 'That's Charlie Roades's horse! Charlie's tied over the saddle! He's dead, Ben!'

'What?' Ben exclaimed.

'Charlie Roades—' Leroy stammered.

'I heard you!' Ben cut him off. 'Anybody around? Did you see anyone?' he demanded gruffly.

Leroy shook his head. 'Just the horse and Charlie tied on the saddle like a sack o' taters!'

'Let's get a light and go see,' Ben said, then turned and went back inside to get his slicker and a lantern.

'Son of a bitch!' Ben Seldon gasped when the lantern light fell on the body. 'Let's get this horse inside the barn and get Charlie off him.'

Leroy took hold of the bridle and led the horse inside the barn. 'Look at that,' he said, 'somebody tied the reins

128

to the saddle horn so the horse could move without tangling.'

Ben glared at him. 'No shit! How the hell else would the horse get here? Hall did this, damn his hide! He led that horse until he was close then let it come in on its own.' Ben took a knife from a belted sheath and cut the hobble holding Charlie's hands and feet together. 'Let's get him off, and see to the horse!'

Ben and Wink pulled the corpse off the horse and Leroy busied himself getting off the saddle and bridle then shooed the horse into a stall. He forked in a generous amount of hay, then began wiping its flanks with a feed sack.

Wink was kneeling beside the body. 'He's been dead for a day or so; hell, he's starting to stink.'

'Look at him, he's all stiff; we're going to have a hell of time trying to bury him!' Leroy remarked.

'One thing about you, Leroy,' Ben said, 'you come up with the damnedest brilliant conclusions one could ask for. Leave the body where it is for tonight. Let's get saddled and head on into Baxter Springs.'

'Huh?'

'See if you can understand this, Leroy. Our man Hall killed Charlie, then has seen fit to ride for a day or so dragging Charlie's body around in a miserable downpour. He could have buried the man, or left him to the coyotes and buzzards out on the prairie, without anyone being the wiser; but nooo! He has to bring him all the way back here and rub our noses in it, like you would do to a cat that just shit in the corner! And he has the gall to sneak in here close enough to allow that horse to deliver the body, in the dark of night, for no reason other than to taunt us. So, I'm figuring that he's still around someplace. All his tracks are being washed away as we stand here talking, and we can't exactly track him in the dark anyway. I figure that he'll hole up some place. What would you do if it was you, Leroy, make a camp on the prairie?' Ben sneered.

Leroy thought for a moment then shook his head. 'A man can't sleep in a rainstorm without protection. I reckon I'd go into Baxter Springs and get myself a room or at least sleep in the livery where it's dry.'

'That's why we're going in! We're gonna check every damned saloon, hotel, livery and flop house that we can find. He's got to spend the night some place. Best be on your toes; that bastard has already killed three men, that we know of. He's pretty damn shrewd, I'll give him that. He's got guts too. Here we were chasing him and now he's turned it around. He knows there's some after him, but he ain't running scared like I figured he would. Instead, the son-of-a-bitch has come after us! Now, let's get into town!' he commanded.

Wink Robbins thought about what Ben had just said for a moment, as he swung his saddle upon his horse's back. It was evident that Sam Hall hadn't come all this way after them, as Ben had put it: the man had come here after Ben Seldon, Wink concluded. He didn't say anything as he cinched the saddle tight.

CHAPTER 20

Sam didn't know that he was so hungry until the aroma of the stew wafted through the air. He wolfed two helpings of stew, some greens and cornbread covered in butter and was working on his third cup of coffee. Now he sat in a stuffed chair supping the coffee, completely content. He knew his body was tired, but he was wide awake from the excitement of getting Charlie Roades's horse to do just as he had figured the animal would do, and then he and Miriam stealing away from danger, without being noticed, still had his blood pumping at his temples.

Oh, but he would have loved to have seen the reaction on their faces when they learned what was on that horse's back. He and Miriam had stayed quietly at a distance long enough to see someone come out of the house with a lantern and move along out toward the corral. It was comical to watch, as suddenly the lantern fell into the mud and then a second time before the man started screeching in front of the house. Sam grinned and could only imagine the consternation and cussing that ensued soon after.

'You can light up if you want to, Sam; Horace always did right after he had a meal,' Miriam called from the kitchen. Sam pulled a muslin sack from his shirt pocket and rolled a smoke then scratched a Lucifer on his boot heel and lit up. Miriam came into the room carrying a coffee cup of her own and seated herself on the sofa.

'I want to thank you for all you've done, Miriam,' Sam began. 'I'm not sure I could have done it without your help. I am indebted to you.'

Miriam smiled. 'You don't owe me a thing Sam, I was happy to help out and I'll tell you why. It all began years ago.' She hesitated for a moment and took a sip of her coffee before continuing. 'It was twenty-six years ago when Horace, my husband, and I came out here and started this farm. The Seldons showed up next door within the year and began building their house. Horace and I helped out when we could. Maggie and George brought Ben along, George's son by his first wife. Ben was just a lad of about ten then. He was big for his age and was good help to George with the chores. J.D. wasn't even born yet. Maggie gave birth to him two years later.

'We got along fine with George and Maggie and shared many a meal in this house and theirs too. A cholera outbreak back in '60 claimed both George and Maggie. Ben was about twenty by then and J.D. was nine, I believe. Horace and I opened up our house to the boys and invited them over often. Ben took his folks' passing pretty hard. He started drinking a lot with a bunch of lowlifes in town and pulled himself into a shell. Being of a big size, he began bullying others and I heard that he was picking fights and carousing almost daily.

132

'He stopped coming around and was distant when we would go over to check on J.D. and him. I don't know how they got by because Ben let the place run down and didn't bother tilling any fields. Now that I look back on it, I guess he had already turned to nighttime thievery in order to sustain himself and J.D. We'd heard of travelers' camps being robbed at night and then some of our cattle, along with the Morrisons', that's the farm on north of here, came up missing. The cattle had obviously been stolen and Horace and Hank Morrison spent three days trying to track them before they gave up. Horace went to see the marshal in Baxter Springs but he couldn't do anything other than saying he'd take it up with the county sheriff. Nothing ever got done about it so we let it go.

'We didn't consider that Ben would stoop to steal from his neighbors, but I believe that we were wrong, though it was never proven. He kept his distance from us and we respectfully kept ours. One day, when J.D. was about seventeen, Horace caught him attempting to brand one of our calves. He had it thrown on its side, tied up and had traced an 'S' on one side. Horace and I joked later if the 'S' stood for Seldon or stolen. Horace went straight over to see Ben. He was given a mild apology, Ben saying it must have been a mistake on J.D.'s part and that he would see to it that it didn't happen again. Within the week when Horace's horse had come home without him, Luther went looking and found Horace lying in a creek with the side of his head caved in. Doctor Grimes, over in Baxter Springs, said he died quickly from the fracture. I told the marshal about the branding incident just a few days before but he discounted any accusations that I might have made against

Ben or J.D. by writing out a report that Horace had died after being thrown from his horse. It might have been the case, but most folks, when thrown from a horse, end up striking their head in the back or front. Even Dr Grimes said it was real unusual that the injury on the side of Horace's head was from a fall from a horse.'

Sam had sat listening to Miriam's rant and felt genuine sympathy for the woman. 'So you think maybe either Ben or J.D. killed Horace and arranged it to look like an accident?'

Miriam nodded. 'I surely do. At first I hated to think of it, but it just kept coming back to me what the doctor had said. And then there was the way Ben and J.D. acted afterwards; they didn't bother to attend the funeral and would purposely cross over the street in town, if they saw me walking along.'

'Have you talked to any other law enforcement people?' Sam asked.

'Yes, I talked to a US marshal over in Joplin. He was sympathetic but indicated that it would be next to impossible to prove foul play unless there was a witness or if someone would confess to the deed.'

Sam nodded. 'I'm sorry for your loss.'

'Thanks. When I first saw that body tied on the horse down in the ravine, I was a little sceptical and wondered what I had walked into but when you told me who it was under that blanket and what you were doing here, I just knew that this was my chance, after all this time, to find out what had really happened to Horace. It's been six years since his passing. Ben's the only one who might know how Horace died, now that J.D. is gone. I'd do about anything to get Ben to open up and confess that it was either J.D. or him who did it out of spite. I could even live with it if he said he didn't know and it was truly an accident, but I won't rest until I know for sure. I'm willing to help you in any way that I can, Sam, in order to accomplish that.'

Miriam paused for a moment to sip from her cup then lowered her eyes to the floor. 'I hope I don't sound too selfish in attempting to use you because, well, oh for goodness sake – yes, I am trying to use you to get what I want. In return you can use my place here to lie low while you figure out how to go about finishing your business. Treat the place as your own, but you'll most likely have to stay out of sight during the day. Lots of eyes in this open country.'

Sam hadn't thought about what he was going to do afterwards. He had been so intent on getting Roades delivered to Ben Seldon's doorstep that he had put any other plans of action out of his mind, figuring to handle things as they came. He could see now that it would have been a foolish move to show up in Baxter Springs. It would have been easy enough for Ben and his group to corner him there and finish him off.

'I came here to get some answers myself. I do hope that you learn what happened to your husband, Miriam. I can see how it would bother a person not to know the truth, particularly when it comes to a loved one's death. I wouldn't get my hopes up too high, if I were you. I am not a fast-draw man, nor have I ever purposefully intended to kill anyone. I'm kind of a victim of circumstance. The killing I've done is because those men were trying to kill me. I just reacted to the situation in the only way I could. You must know that when there's a shootout, there may not be a chance to just wing the other person. It's good odds that someone is going to go down and with the size of bullets these guns are shooting, if a man gets hit by one of them, then he's most likely going to die right soon. You'll be taking a big risk by hiding me out. If Ben Seldon learns of it, he's apt to do something mean and nasty. Who knows, he might try to burn you out, or even to do you in.'

'I'm willing to take that chance, Sam,' Miriam assured him.

'What about this fella Luther that you speak of?' Sam asked.

Miriam smiled. 'Luther is my brother. He doesn't live in the house; never has since we brought him here. Luther prefers to sleep in the bunkhouse we have next door. He was badly wounded in the war by an explosion. He lost part of his left leg; he gets around with a wooden peg strapped to his stump.

'By the time the war ended we hadn't heard from Luther in over two years and feared the worst. When we had word that he was in the Gratiot Street prison in St Louis, Horace and I went to see if and when he could be released.

'Apparently they were anxious for our arrival and quickly agreed to discharge Luther into our care. The reason was soon apparent: Luther's mind had been addled by the same explosion that had taken his lower leg. One of the guards at the prison even went so far as to say that Luther was crazy. Well, he's not crazy. He may have had a few peculiarities at the time seeing how they had

136

him locked away in a crowded cell where he languished in a bunk most of the time. The only attempt to help him was to provide a wooden stick, at mealtimes, to use as a crutch to get around. We brought Luther here and he settled right in, but refused to live in the house with Horace and me, preferring instead to live in the bunkhouse Horace had built for hired hands. He has moments when he regresses to the fighting and sometimes he acts like a twelve-year-old child; otherwise he lives a peaceful life and works hard at keeping this place up particularly since Horace's passing. He'll be sleeping now, but you can get acquainted tomorrow. There's another bunk in the bunkhouse that you can use. And don't worry, Luther is not dangerous to be around.'

CHAPTER 21

While Ben Seldon, Wink Robbins and Leroy Hagen were canvassing Baxter Springs in hopes of finding Sam Hall, Nick Shores and Rob Bonhart had ridden in to the Seldon place. Both men were sitting in the house drinking whiskey when Ben Seldon rode in.

Ben noticed the two extra horses in the barn when he was putting his horse away for the night. He smiled broadly. 'Good, they are just in time to help us flush Sam Hall out of hiding,' he muttered, while pulling the saddle from his horse.

Nick and Rob were sitting at the table when Ben walked in. Rob was a tall man who carried his 165 pound weight well, being broad-shouldered and slim of hips. He held a neat appearance as if he cared about his looks and his clothes. He had dark hair and mustache and wore knee-high boots with his trouser legs tucked inside. On his hip was a .44 Colt nestled in a polished holster tied down to his thigh. Seemingly a quiet man, there was an imposing air about him, particularly if you looked into his dark eyes. If a man were to stand before him in belligerence, a look into those eyes might save the opposition's life if he lived long enough to suddenly reconsider.

Nick Shores was almost the exact opposite of his partner, being short of stature: five foot six and a beefy 170 pounds. He looked and talked like he was raised in a low-class saloon. His clothes looked as if he had slept in them and his boots were scarred and worn at the heel from long use and neglect. Nick was the talker of the two and he didn't mind running off at the mouth about any subject. He would be the first to tell you if he figured you had stepped into his territory.

Both men had taken off their hats, the lamplight giving a shine to their hair where it had been matted down by their hats.

'Glad you could make it, Nick, Rob. We've been expecting you all evening,' Ben said.

'We got in a couple hours ago. We saw Charlie Roades's body in the barn. Somebody sure as hell shot him dead. Was it Sam Hall who did it?' Nick asked.

Ben was taking off his slicker. He had one arm out and one still in the armhole, and paused before pulling the dripping slicker the rest of the way off. 'I'm sure he did. Charlie's horse came in on its own with Charlie tied on its back shortly after dark. He couldn't have done that if it were much of a distance. I thought it was you and Rob coming in when I first heard the horse. It looks like Charlie has been dead for a day or so. We couldn't track in the dark and rain so we went into Baxter Springs hoping to catch up to that son of a bitch Hall. He's too slick though; nobody in town has seen hide nor hair of him. I left Wink and Leroy in town in case he comes in tonight looking for a place to sleep. It's pretty damn miserable out in the rain. Maybe it will stop and we can pick up a track or so in the morning.'

Nick Shores took hold of the bottle on the table and pulled out the cork with a squeak. He hefted it to Rob, who was stubbing out the pinched end of a cigarette in a tomato can. When Rob shook his head, Nick refilled his own cup then handed the bottle to Ben. Ben had hung up his slicker and taken a chair nearby.

'So you figure that this guy Hall killed Charlie then delivered his body to you?' Nick asked.

Ben took a long draught of the whiskey bottle. 'That's what it looks like to me. If anybody else had shot Charlie they would've just left him lie.'

Nick stood then paced a step or two toward the door then turned back. He cleared his throat to get Ben's attention. He'd worked for and with Ben before and things had not worked out exactly as he had figured when it came time to splitting up money from a job. Nick was now wary of the words spoken in that saloon in Joplin about Ben's offer of $1,000 for the capture or killing of Sam Hall. It sounded pretty good in the lamplight of the saloon while the drinks were flowing freely but now it appeared things were not quite the same. He intended to make sure things were spelled out prior to setting out on a job.

'Hell, Ben, this kinda changes the game a little bit,' he said hesitantly, not wanting to get Ben's dander up.

Ben looked up, his eyes narrowing inquisitively. 'How's that?'

'Over in Joplin, you said Rob and I would be trailing Hall once you found out where the man had taken off to. Rob and I were all set to make a run down into Texas, catch up with Hall and bring him back to you for the reward. The two of us could make do real well in a split of the money. Now that the man has gone and showed up hereabouts, who's to say which man's gun does the killing? I mean, you're trying to shoot him; you got Wink and Leroy out trying to shoot him, and you want Rob and me to get after him too! Are you going to pay shares to me and Rob if you and two others are shooting at the same time? It appears to me that the value has gone down some. We didn't come in on this hunt just to get grub and wages to get by on, like Wink and Leroy do.'

Ben had never minced his words to anyone, usually not giving a damn what they thought, but now it seemed he was stumped as he stared at the floor for a moment. 'I guess I hadn't thought about it like that.' He stood, swigged the whiskey, then wiped his mouth with the back of his hand before setting the bottle on to the table. 'Hell, I never figured you boys would ride for nothing. Tell you what I'll do: I'll give you and Rob a hundred apiece, right now, if you'll stick around and help to locate Hall. Once we tag him I'll put up another hundred apiece whether it's your shot that gets him or not. 'Course if you and Rob are out on your own and happen to get him then I'll still pay the thousand like I said I would. Minus the two hundred you already got. What do you say?'

Nick looked at Rob and the two men nodded to each other. 'I reckon that we can live with that, Ben. We'll give it a week and see how it goes.' Nick said.

'Fine, fine,' Ben said, then went to the satchel in which he kept his coins and began counting out five twenty-dollar gold pieces for each man.

CHAPTER 22

The inside of the bunkhouse smelled of tobacco smoke and kerosene. Sam wasn't sure if it was the odor from the lit lamp that he had brought in with him, or older fumes from Luther's use earlier. The usual stink of cows, men's sweat and dirty socks wasn't there, the room had a wooden floor that was neat and clean. Overall it was dry and warmed by a small stove at the far end.

There was a table in the middle of the room where he set the lamp. On the far wall were two bunks, the lower one being occupied by Luther who was sound asleep. His shirt and pants were hung on pegs driven into the bed post. A lone boot and an eighteen inch peg with leather strapping attached to it set before the bunk. Behind the door was another set of bunks across from where Luther lay. Sam set his rifle next to the lower bunk. He made short work of shucking his boots and still wet to damp clothes, draping them over a chair to dry, then pulled the quilt back from the already made bunk. He blew out the lamp then stepped to the bunk and slid in. He was so exhausted that he was asleep by the time his head hit the pillow.

Sam woke up to sunlight shining through a window at the foot of his bunk. He lay there looking at the rays as an occasional sparkle from the little motes of dust that hung in the air bounced around. He was grateful that the rain had finally stopped. Feeling eyes on him, he turned his head to see a man sitting at the table puffing a pipe. Blue smoke curled from his mouth. He was a slight man of fifty or so years with thinned gray hair.

'Good morning, Sam. I'm Luther. Miriam told me about you. Said you'd be with us for a spell. I expect she'll be bringing our breakfast in right soon.'

Sam pulled back the quilt and swung around to sit on the edge of the bunk.

' 'Morning, Luther. I'm pleased to meet you. If she's coming down, I reckon I'd best get dressed.' He put on his socks then stood and pulled on his pants. His clothes had dried in the warm room. He stuffed his shirt into his pants, tightened his belt, then sat and pulled on his boots, then walked over and stuck out his hand for a shake. Luther shook, then said, 'Privy's not too far.' He pointed the stem of his pipe in the direction of the little building just off from the corral and barn.

'Thanks,' Sam said, then disappeared out the door.

By the time Sam came back into the bunkhouse, Miriam had just finished setting out dishes for a setting of three. She had brought a pot of coffee and poured a cup for Luther and another for Sam. 'You men have a little coffee while I bring in breakfast.' She disappeared, but was back soon with a cloth-covered platter of bacon, eggs and pancakes.

After everyone had helped themselves they ate mostly

in silence until Luther asked, 'Where you from, Sam?'

'Texas. I was born and raised there on a small ranch.'

'Ah, then you are a cowboy. You sure got the look. We used to see lots of them a while back when the herds came through, but not so much anymore.'

'I reckon you could say that,' Sam admitted. 'I expect to go back home after a bit.'

'Sam will be with us for a while, Luther.' Miriam interrupted. 'He's our guest, but we don't want anyone to know that he is here. There are some bad men who would do harm to him, if they knew of his whereabouts.' Luther nodded his understanding of what was said, but remained silent. Sam was grateful to Miriam for breaking in and saving him from having to explain things all over again, but he wondered if her speaking to Luther as a mother would a child, was perhaps being a little over protective of the man. He seemed perfectly coherent to Sam. Well, he wasn't about to get involved in any family business, so he just smiled agreeably while forking some pancake into his mouth.

Sam spent the rest of the morning mostly inside the barn. He curried the roan and rechecked all his gear. When that was done he searched for any undone chores that needed doing. He was able to fork some hay to a milk cow and four head of horses lazing in the corral but found little else to do. Luther spent his days fixing anything needed doing and it appeared that he was caught up on his chores. By nightfall Sam was tired out from just lazing about. He lay on the bunk thinking of what to do next. He didn't come here to hide out. If he showed himself to the pack over at Seldon's place they would attack with a vengeance. It was time to find out how many men were over there and figure out how to begin picking them off one at a time, if he could. He did not want to endanger Miriam and Luther in any way, so he would have to continue to work in stealth. He napped for two or three hours then got up around midnight. Carefully, and as quietly as he could, Sam tiptoed out of the bunkhouse then went into the barn. He saddled his horse, checked the loads in his six-gun and his saddle gun. He blew out the lantern he was using, then mounted, trying to walk the horse slowly without it clomping its feet.

Under a silvery quarter moon he guided his horse back to the ravine where he had first taken sanctuary. From here he could follow the creek in a south-easterly route for a few miles without leaving many tracks back the way he had come in. He travelled all the way to the road that led to Baxter Springs. He rode that west until he found a road heading north. He took it and was able to come into Seldon's place from the south. It seemed a long way to travel if one was going from Miriam Holder's place to Ben Seldon's, but this way the only tracks anyone would be able to follow would lead only to Baxter Springs and away from the Holder ranch.

Sam had gotten as close as he dared on horseback. In the moonlight he could see the buildings in the distance, maybe 500 yards away, but wasn't close enough to see how many head of horses were there. Plenty of water gorged out ravines around, so he led his roan into one and tied the reins to a nearby bush. He slid the Henry out of the boot and took off on foot toward the buildings.

There were eight horses in the corral, but inside the

darkened barn he was able to locate, only six saddles were strung out on the stalls. One of the saddles he figured as belonging to Charlie Roades so that meant there were five men inside the house. Five against one were the odds against him right now. He wanted to leave a calling card of some sort, so he cut into the cinch on each saddle: there would be no quick mounting and riding off. When finished, Sam crept outside then made his way back.

Sam was in the bunkhouse just as a yellowing was beginning to show on the eastern horizon. Miriam didn't say anything at breakfast, but Sam figured she was aware of his nocturnal riding. It was afterwards when Sam was tending to his horse that Miriam came into the barn.

'Couldn't sleep, Sam?'

'I was just doing a little investigating.' He told her of the route he had taken in order to keep his whereabouts and her involvement anonymous.

'You don't have to get in any hurry about it, Sam, there's time,' Miriam said.

Sam nodded. 'Putting it off never makes things any better. I can't go through life waiting on what Ben Seldon might or might not do. He's here and I'm here! I'm going to force the issue and deal with it here and now. I'll work at night; it's the only cover I have.'

Sam slept until about 2 p.m. when he was shaken awake by Luther who put a finger to his lips then pointed outside. Obviously he wanted Sam to be quiet and peek outside.

Luther then thumped his stump as he walked to the door and outside to stand on the little porch while looking at a mounted man. Sam stood near the door with his gun in hand and watched through a crack in the door frame.

Nick Shores sat on his horse while his eyes searched. Miriam had come out of the house and stood at the bottom of the porch steps looking up at the mounted man.

'I'm with a group; we're looking for a man who's got a bounty on him. He could be dangerous,' Nick stated flatly then demanded, 'How about you, peg leg, have you seen any strangers around the last day or so?'

Sam watched as Luther shook his head. 'No, no strangers here; what's this fella that you're looking for done?'

Nick Shores looked off as if unconcerned, then spat a gob of tobacco juice on to the ground. 'He's a killer and we aim to put a stop to him before he does it again. You see anything, we're over to Ben's place.' His voice was trailing off as he turned his horse and rode away.

When Shores was well gone, Sam walked over to Miriam who was watching the man ride toward Seldon's. 'He or one of the others may be back. Near as I could tell there are five of them. That's how many saddles I found other than Charlie's. It's possible that they figured out that I wasn't in Baxter Springs and the only possibility left was that I was holed up at one of the neighboring spreads. If things get too hot around here, Miriam, I'll leave before I bring any harm your way.'

Miriam nodded. 'I think you're doing it the right way, Sam. I also believe that the man who was here, or the others in his bunch, wouldn't hesitate to shoot you if they could.'

Sam waited until it was well after dark before he readied

to take off again. He did not have a specific plan of action to follow, but figured that nothing would get done unless he could get close to the others and see of their actions; perhaps overhear a conversation as to their plans.

He took the same route that he had taken the previous night and it did not seem to take as long this time. He tied the horse then crept along in the moonlight toward the buildings.

He was a hundred yards away kneeling behind a bush when he saw the flare of a match as someone lit up a smoke near the corner of the barn. When the flare died away, he could see the tip of the tobacco stick glowing orange. He watched the glow increase from time to time as the man sucked on it. It was obvious they had posted a lookout since his raid last night, but the man was not watching very well. Sam was able to clearly see what the posted man was doing, but it was obvious that the lookout was totally unaware of Sam's presence. This man lounging in the darkness was alone and that gave Sam an advantage and an idea. All he had to do was to use stealth, the darkness, and surprise to overcome and eliminate this lone wolf.

If he were discovered the whole group would come down on him. He tried to figure a way to render him helpless without killing him, but even if he merely knocked the man out, Sam figured he would be up and back after him come daylight. No, if he wanted to end this chase then this man needed to be eliminated. Perhaps he could capture him, but to do that silently was taking a big chance. He didn't like killing, but sometimes it had to be done for the good of others.

He remembered when he was a kid of twelve and his father had cut a hog's throat. 'That pig would lie around here forever expecting to be fed. It's either you spend your time catering to him or fix him for your own use,' his father had said. 'It is best for us if this is done.'

It took Sam fifteen minutes of carefully slow movements to get into position. He stood near the darkened corner of the barn wall, trying not to breathe, sure that his own thudding heartbeat could be heard. When the flare of another fired match brightened just around the corner confirmed the man was still there, Sam stepped forward quickly and around the corner throwing a hard sucker punch to the man's surprised face, connecting with his jaw, followed up with another punch to the man's belly.

Surprisingly, instead of going down, as Sam expected, the man went on the attack swinging a meaty fist at Sam that connected with the side of Sam's head and staggered him. Sam reflexed immediately by swinging his fist. He felt his fist meet Nick Shores' head, right on his ear. The blow knocked Shores' hat off. Nick Shores pulled a knife from a sheath and lunged at Sam. Moonlight glinted off the blade as the man bulled forward, intent on stabbing the blade into Sam's middle. Sam jumped aside at a critical moment and delivered a fist to the back of the man's head. Shores staggered forward and head butted the barn. Sam punched a murderous punch to the man's kidney area. It was enough to make Shores drop the knife then make a move for his gun. Sam batted a hand at Shores' hand to knock it away then reached down and scooped up the knife.

Nick grunted like a pig when Sam shoved the knife into

the small of his back. Sam could smell the man's sweat and tobacco as he pushed the knife in Nick's back until he heard the air escaping from the stricken man's lungs. He waited until the man's arms had dropped and all movement had ceased, then let him down to the ground, leaving the knife sticking in his back. Sam was fearful of others overhearing the commotion. He looked about anxiously with his gun at the ready but no one seemed to have heard. Rattled by the encounter, Sam left by the way he had come in.

CHAPTER 23

It was 4 a.m. when Wink Robbins, Nick Shores' lookout relief, discovered the body. Within minutes Ben Seldon and the others were all standing around looking at the body under the lantern light. 'Damn, I hate to see that,' Rob Bonhart lamented. 'We've been riding together for a couple years now.' He pulled out the knife, wiping the blade on Nick's shirt. 'This man Hall ain't so easy to catch.'

'That bastard is gonna get us all!' Leroy Hagen whined.

'No, he ain't!' Ben Seldon exclaimed. 'Soon as it's daylight, we're going to cover every damn inch of this place until we find sign, then we're going to track him right back to where he's hiding.' Ben bent over the body and searched around until he found the five pieces of gold that he had paid out to Nick. He stuffed them into his pocket. 'He didn't earn it and won't have a need for it!' he said, then stood. 'Let's get him into the barn. Leroy, you can dig him a grave later on.'

Leroy dropped his arms in disgust. 'How come I got to dig him a grave? Hell, Rob's his partner. I had to dig that

151

big hole to put Charlie's crooked body in, and we ain't exactly got any coffin-making boards. I used what was lying around to build one for Charlie.'

Ben turned on Leroy in a fury. 'By damn you'll dig that hole because I said so! I'm damned tired of your sniffling and whining. You don't need any coffin boards; just put him in a hole and cover him up – unless you want to invite the parson in town to say a few words and you might just as well bring on a church choir to boot!'

CHAPTER 24

It was near four o'clock and Sam had been awake for a while so decided to get up. Luther wasn't in the bunkhouse which meant that he was out doing a chore someplace. Sam walked over to the house to scrounge a cup of coffee. At the same time Miriam was standing at a kitchen window looking out when she saw a tall man wearing knee-high boots and holding a gun creeping along the back of the bunkhouse. Before she could react Sam had passed the corner when Rob Bonhart stepped out behind him. Sam heard the metallic click as Rob cocked his weapon.

'Don't make a move or I'll plug you,' he instructed. Sam froze and began to raise his hands. 'It took me a while but I followed your tracks right up that creek all the way from the road. Now we're going over to see Ben Seldon—'

Whack! was the sound of a shovel batting off the back of Rob Bonhart's head. He fell towards Sam who moved and let him fall to the ground. Luther stood there holding the shovel in his hand.

'Thanks!' Sam said, then reached down and took Rob

Bonhart's gun from his hand.

Miriam came rushing out of the front door, 'Sam, are you OK?' she said, excitedly. 'I saw that man sneaking around from my kitchen window, but couldn't warn you in time?'

'Yeah, I'm OK. Looks like one of them tracked me down. I'll get some rope and tie him up,' He hurried off to get some rope to tie Bonhart's hands behind his back. When he awoke and was sitting with his back to the bunkhouse wall he asked, 'Are you Hall?'

'How many are out looking for me?' When Rob didn't answer, Sam gave the man's booted foot a kick with his own. 'You didn't shoot me because you weren't sure who you had covered, so I won't shoot you in a place that's lethal, but I can make things awfully uncomfortable for you unless you answer me!' He placed his pistol next to one of Bonhart's legs then pulled back the hammer.

Rob squirmed in an attempt to move his leg away then said, 'No need for that! I figure you'd do it. There's just Ben, myself and two others left. You killed my partner last night!'

'Do they know that you're over here?' Sam asked.

Rob shook his head. 'I don't think so. They are out looking like I was doing.'

'What time you figure Ben will be there to accept visitors?' Sam asked.

'I don't know; anytime now I expect, but I don't know Ben or his habits, my partner knew him but I didn't. We were just in it for the money. You let me go, Hall, and I'll ride on. I got no quarrel with you.'

Sam shook his head. 'Five minutes ago you were all set

to take me out and collect the reward for yourself. So, why don't we go on over and see Ben right now?'

Sam looked over to Miriam. 'Would you be interested in delivering this yahoo back to Ben?'

'What do you have in mind, Sam?' she asked.

'We take your wagon; put him in the bed. You drive in like the concerned neighbor that you are but I'll be in the bed also. When Ben comes out, I'll confront him. In other words, I'm proposing to end this today – right now. You might be able to learn of your husband's mishap. What do you say?'

Miriam thought for only a moment before she declared, 'Yes, let's do it!'

Sam, with Luther's help, harnessed a team and brought the wagon around. Rob was thrown into the back of the wagon while Miriam climbed into the driver's seat. Sam marveled as Luther handed a double-barreled Greener shotgun up to Miriam, then had somehow managed to climb a wheel and seated himself next to her.

Sam asked, 'You sure you want to go along, Luther?'

The man nodded. 'It needs to get done,' he said.

Sam checked his gun loads then crawled into the wagon and lay down beside Rob. He pulled his gun and stuck it in Rob's side, 'Just lie still. You even think of trying to alert them and I'll drop the hammer!'

The trip to Ben Seldon's seemed like it took an hour, though it was only two miles and actually took less than ten minutes to get there. Miriam snapped a rein now and then to get the team to march right up into Ben Seldon's yard. Ben came out first and stood on the porch to watch as the wagon approached. He was followed by Wink Robbins who stood menacingly to Ben's right. Leroy Hagen had just walked over from the corral to stand to the right, but in front of Wink. The porch was elevated about two feet off the ground.

When Miriam pulled the team to a stop, Ben had an inquisitive look on his face as he stared at his neighbors. The angle was enough that he could not see Rob Bonhart and Sam Hall lying in the bed of the wagon behind those on the seat. When Miriam had finished tying the reins to a brake handle and looked up, Ben spoke, 'Miriam, Luther, what brings you over?'

'We're just delivering your man back to you, Ben.' Miriam said.

Ben looked at her. 'Wha—?' he started to say, then stopped and said instead, 'Leroy, go over there, and see what she's talking about!' When Leroy took a step forward, Luther elevated the shotgun to point at the man.

As if on cue, Sam suddenly rose up and heaved himself over the side of the wagon to land on his feet facing the men.

Leroy came to an abrupt stop when he saw the shotgun, then he waved his hand at Sam, 'That's him! That's Hall! Ben! That's him!'

Ben's eyes flared. 'I heard you, Leroy!' He pointed a finger. 'Well, well, looks like we don't have to look no more. So you're the great Sam Hall, bounty hunter and murdering scum! What are you doing here, Hall, looking to collect your own bounty? Tired of me chasing you? I would have caught you sooner or later!'

Sam stood unflinching, hands at his side. 'I come to tell you that I was in a card game in Ellsworth with a man they say was your brother. He tried to draw down on me for no good reason. We fought. His own gun went off between us and he took the bullet. Later, that man' – he pointed at Leroy Hagan – 'and another, drew on me and my partner. He shot my partner Daniel, while Daniel shot the other man. My gun was lost in the scuffle with J.D. and I didn't do any of the shooting. The law said that J.D.'s death was done in self-defense and paid me a reward that I was not after. I didn't purposely go looking for J.D. like you've had others looking for me. I've come to see if you can be reasonable enough to understand that I did not murder him. I'm here to end this, one way or the other! I won't run.'

Ben flared his arm around. 'You've come to the right place and we got you outnumbered!'

'I don't think so, Seldon,' Sam said. 'For one thing the three of you can try to shoot me down and you might do it, but I'll at least get you with my first shot; maybe one other with the second, and the Greener will take care of the third! It doesn't have to be this way! It's up to you, you can call it off!' Then Sam directed a question to Leroy Hagen and Wink Robbins while keeping his eyes riveted on Seldon, 'You men, who's going to pay you when Ben goes down? And he will get my first shot unless he calls an end to this bounty business!'

Wink Robbins was not one to back down from a fight if the odds favored him, but it didn't take a genius to figure the odds against a double- barreled Greener and a man known to be fast on the draw to convince him to slowly raise his hands. 'He's making sense, Ben!' Wink said.

Ben glanced over at him. 'The hell you say!' he yelled, then made a move for his gun. Sam drew his weapon and fired. The front of Ben's shirt moved as if a wind were blowing when the bullet caught him in the stomach. He staggered back, but was trying to raise his gun to fire and step forward at the same time when Sam shot him again. Leroy Hagen had dived to the ground, arms stretched out, without drawing his six-gun. Wink Robbins stood with raised hands. Ben had dropped his gun never having fired the weapon. He slumped back against the door and slid down.

Sam turned his weapon toward Wink Robbins who still had his hands up. 'Pitch your pistol to the ground!' Sam ordered. 'Careful!' Wink reached down slowly and withdrew the gun from his holster using his thumb and forefinger. He lifted it gingerly, holding it out, as if it were a varmint that could bite, then, by the flip of a wrist, tossed it to the ground. Sam walked over to Leroy Hagen who was still lying on the ground. He fished Leroy's gun from his holster. 'You come down from the porch and the two of you stand still until I've finished here.' Wink Robbins went over to stand next to Leroy under the watchful eye of Luther, who covered the pair with the shotgun.

Miriam climbed down and scurried to kneel beside Seldon. Ben's eyes were open and he attempted a smile when Miriam took one of his hands in hers. 'Ben, tell me what happened to Horace? Please, Ben, I need to know,' she pleaded.

Sam knelt beside her.

Ben's eyes rolled back in his head and he closed his eyes. Sam shook him and slapped at his face. 'Ben, wake up!' Ben opened his eyes. His face was pasty and there was blood covering his chest where he had taken the second bullet as well as his stomach where the first one had hit. His breathing was awkward – a short breath wheezed out, then, after a struggle for another, he seemed to be relieved somewhat. Sam looked into his eyes. 'I didn't want to shoot you or those others you sent after me, but you gave me no choice.'

Ben nodded. 'J.D. was my only kin, I – I had to do it,' he muttered.

'No, you didn't, you could have listened to reason,' Sam said. Ben fluttered his eyes but didn't attempt to answer.

'You haven't got long, Seldon,' Sam told him. Ben's eyes were clouded with pain but they registered the inevitable. Sam prodded some more. 'Miriam has been a good neighbor and she cared for you, your brother and your folks. I think they would all want you to tell her what you know about her husband?'

Ben's eyes opened fully and his lips began to move but nothing came out, then he gasped a short breath and began to mutter. 'J.D. hit him. I had told him to forget about Horace catching him with the calf, but J.D. wouldn't let it go. I had to protect J.D. He was just a kid. I couldn't stand by and let the law haul him off to hang!'

'We'll get you a doctor, Ben,' Miriam said, while tears streamed down her face.

Ben nodded. 'I'm sorry about Horace.' A flood of blood erupted from his mouth. He coughed once and attempted a breath but only blood and air wheezed out instead. Ben's legs twitched and his eyes remained open and fixed in a death stare. Miriam touched both eyes to close them, then stood.

Sam, Miriam and Luther herded Wink Robbins, Rob

Bonhart and Leroy Hagen to the marshal's office in Baxter Springs.

'Miriam, I'm satisfied that Horace's death was caused by J.D. and that chapter is closed,' the marshal said. 'The Seldons have been a pain to this community for a long time; too bad they had to involve Sam Hall and cause all this killing. But they both came to an end that they surely deserved.'

Two days had passed since Seldon's death. Leroy Hagen was retained in jail to account for the dodger of $200 on him. Wink Robbins and Rob Bonhart were released but ordered to leave the county.

Sam was rested and ready to leave when he led his horse to stand in the yard as Miriam and Luther came out to see him off.

'I can't thank you enough, Miriam, and you too, Luther,' Sam said.

'Oh, but it is I who thank you, Sam,' Miriam said. 'Now that I know what actually happened to Horace I can rest easier at night. Don't be a stranger, Sam, we'd like to see you again. You are welcome here. Where are you off to now that you are free?' Miriam asked.

'I've some unfinished business with a lady in Wichita. Any plans beyond that will depend on what she says,' Sam said, with a big smile on his face, as he swung into his saddle and rode off.